The Years of Chaos

The YEARS of CHAOS

Every circumstances and bruises
have an unresolved past.

Reine Backoulas-Zenta

iUniverse, Inc.
Bloomington

The Years of Chaos
Every circumstances and bruises have an unresolved past.

iUniverse books may be ordered through booksellers or by contacting:

iUniverse
1663 Liberty Drive
Bloomington, IN 47403
www.iuniverse.com
1-800-Authors (1-800-288-4677)

ISBN: 978-1-4620-2361-5 (sc)
ISBN: 978-1-4620-2362-2 (e)

Printed in the United States of America

iUniverse rev. date: 06/15/2011

Sebastian Langes was his name, that was what he told me on the day our paths crossed. It was early in August, and the warm, hot sun seemed to enliven the streets we walked upon.

Sebastian was a soldier—but not just any kind of soldier. He was a great and rare kind of soldier, back during a time when soldiers were truly worshiped and highly respected. I remember clearly the day Sebastian and I first met, as if it just happened. Sebastian told me arrogantly, in accurate detail, about every woman he had been with in his early twenties; according to him, they had all told him how desirable and handsome he was. Sebastian never hesitated to brag to me about how many women he had been with in every place and every corner of the world he had traveled to.

The name Sebastian, yes, that name. It is a name that haunted me whenever I heard it. The name Sebastian was practically banned from ever being mentioned in my presence again. However, the name also carried special memories with it. Those memories were still living with me, and I was unable to let them just die and bury them once and for all.

Only a couple of weeks after I met Sebastian, we discovered the enormous feelings we had developed for each other. After just six months, I was overwhelmed by all his expectations; if there was something Sebastian knew how to do, it was to take from others without ever having to return the favor later on. He never took any kind of precaution, nor did he have any sort of reservation when he spoke about himself, his past, and his family. At times, it appeared as if he loved himself more than he loved anyone else.

He was raised by his mother, who divorced his father only a few weeks after he was born. Sebastian's mother always told him that his father was an alcoholic, who profusely abused her physically, mentally, and even sexually whenever no one was around, especially when he was drunk. Sebastian told me his father never went a day without putting his hands around his mother's throat. It was a game for his father to rape and beat his mother, meanwhile he sucked all the tears off her face until they dried out. Sebastian also told me that his father found it pleasurable to see his mother cry out to neighbors for the safety of her own life, not that anyone at that time even cared enough anyway, Sebastian would say.

Sebastian only spoke about his father when I asked about him. On those occasions, he would unhappily exclaim that he did not want to be reminded of his father, who died of an unknown disease. I did, however, find his resentment toward his father both cruel and inhuman, since his father was no longer alive. His repression, whenever he spoke of his family, was too cold for one to ignore.

After being with Sebastian for only six months, Sebastian asked me to become his wife. I agreed to marry him, regardless of his maltreatments toward others, especially women. He had a lot of anger in him and a lot of hate toward young, beautiful women. Sebastian had, for many years, treated women as if they were simply a bunch of whores or, better yet, animals. Despite Sebastian's tendencies to abuse and disrespect women, I believed I was in love; I thought he would change or I could come up with some mysterious ways to change him.

The constant debate about his father began to pull us apart, but that wasn't the cause for our broken engagement, which came after eleven months. I can't exactly remember what Sebastian told me concerning his mother, but he always kept it brief whenever he spoke about her, except when he spoke about her bravery and how she had raised him to be such a good man all on her own.

Sebastian was a peculiar man; after our engagement, he wanted me to marry him as quickly as possible, without saying why. After he proposed to me, he became highly secretive and rarely spoke about himself, his past, his work, nor did he continue to speak of his mother. After we broke our engagement, I thought I would forget him, but I was very wrong to make such an assumption.

I thought about how I had gotten there, but all I could remember was the first time I met Sebastian. He possessed virtue and qualities that one could never imagine. He had such a vibrant presence about him, and he gave an impression of both warmth and reassurance to the weakest hearts, who did not know him well enough. I guess our relationship had been cursed from the beginning; right after we got engaged, his voice got dry; as every day went by, he changed enormously into a cold stranger, and his emotions became overly detached from mine and from this world. His actions became as secretive as that of an old rat; he would hide things away from me, and he'd say that it was none of my concern.

Many questions came in my mind very often, and on many occasions, he acted as though I would be so naïve as to go through with the wedding, marry him, and leave the city in which I was born and raised, a city I grew to love with my complete heart and soul, abandon the only family I have known and loved so dearly, and entrust my entire life and future to a man I barely understood. I was never able to relate any of my feelings to him; he was profusely cold and ruthless, selfish and demanding. I thought at times that the devil himself had been reincarnated inside Sebastian Langes, so he could ruin me and all my precious dreams I had in my mind. My future could not have been as bright and beautiful as one may have believed it to be, since I had grown to be really distant from the exterior world around me.

With time, Sebastian became more vicious than ever, as I got to know him even more. The only thing that pleased him was his endless, cold silence, and the only time he spoke of himself was when he spoke proudly about his long service to the French army, which he served for more than thirteen years, which tended to always give me a painful kick inside my stomach. And yes, the army was indeed all he had known, and it became in time the only subject he spoke about when he was with me. He mentioned the high rank he had achieved when he was still in the French army, he spoke arrogantly about all the beautiful girls he had met during the years he was serving in the army, and he spoke about a particular girl name Jane Claire, who had been very special to him and very close to his heart. He mentioned her quite a lot. He spoke of how he almost married her but failed, because he always feared, once he went to war, that he may not return to her safely.

Sebastian always knew how to fill my head with vague stories, and he knew very well how to bore me whenever he felt the need to do just that. His past appeared to be the present, and the present the future, whenever he talked about it, but I never did believe in any of it; I guess that was just my way of avoiding the chances of being disappointed.

Instead, I found all those stories boring and torturing to both the mind and the soul. I grew more suspicious of his behavior every day, I suspected that he must have had another life, which turned out to be true. Just a few months after I became engaged to him, I opened his briefcase while he was out on a walk and found a notebook with several addresses and a picture of a woman. I was both surprised and confused beyond words by what I had seen; still, I felt it would be wise for me to act as if I had seen nothing at all, so I kept my mouth shut.

When he returned from his walk around seven that night, I asked him to take me home, and later that month, I requested a permanent separation, which he granted—but not so easily. He was enraged by my decision to end it all with him, and he began to fill my mailbox with letters that tended to lower my self-esteem; he spoke of how lousy of a wife I would have made if we had gotten married, and he mocked the poverty of my family in each letter.

Despite Sebastian's intentions to cause me emotional harm, I did not notify anyone about his verbal and physical threats; I thought they would not care as much, especially since he was in the French army. Instead, I responded to each of his letters with a very cold silence. Sebastian, in time, became tired of me not responding to him at all, but I was still carrying his face and inhuman behavior inside my mind. I was in my late twenties at the time, and I was trying to figure out what on earth I was doing with someone who not only used me and destroyed every bit of confidence I had in myself to console his own insecurity, but also terrified me. Sebastian had taken into his advantage every single one of my weaknesses as a source of strength. I became angry and was disappointed with myself. Even though Sebastian was no longer in my life, I couldn't stop feeling that he had won.

After three long seasons of great pain and suffering, then came the spring; all was new again, my life seemed to be rejuvenated, I started going out more often than when I was still with Sebastian. But before I could continue my journey, I knew there was a past in me, other than the one I shared with Sebastian, and I needed to rediscover that past of mine once more, so I could bury all of it once and forever. I went to an isolated park, which was filled with hundreds of trees that had dried over the winter season, and the trees stood tall before me, but carried with them no life at all. Each single one of those trees appeared as dead on the outside as I was in the inside.

I sat upon a big rock, which felt very cold when I sat on it; the rock appeared to have had been unmoved for many years. I began to recall my past, mostly my childhood, until I reached a silent moment, a moment when I became unconscious. In that unconsciousness, with no doubt at all or uncertainty, I walked through the shadow of my own thoughts. *I can now see it all now,* I thought, and suddenly fear began to surround me once more; doubts and regrets about the past filled my heart with great despair and hopelessness as I recalled my past.

I started to ask myself if it had all been for nothing. I continued my unconscious debate in my mind, wondering and asking again and again if there was something, or particularly someone, out there in a hidden place, or inside a forgotten world, waiting for me to act and watching me obsessively go through my inner struggles, while I wandered around like a lost child inside the jungle of the dead.

The promenade inside my head did not end then; I continued to reflect on things that I had failed to love and to appreciate during my childhood. I could clearly see now how blindly I had lived my life for many years. I stood cautiously from where I was sitting; my palms felt cold from what I saw, and I began to walk in silence. My own shadow now consoled me while my mind traveled to a past that was fading away as quickly as a lost dream, yet leaving me with questions that could not be answered. The images I tried to recapture and bring to life could barely reach a clear end, and I had no desire to pursue those images. My heart lacked the power and the passion it needed at the time to see it all once again. Everything I had seen in my past seemed to vanish like the breeze of autumn. My mind became blank, and the image of the past completely faded away, leaving darkness without any light.

I wondered what had happened to the other nine years that my mind could not remember, the nine years of hard work. I asked myself if it had all disappeared somewhere along the path that I had chosen. *My destiny no longer obeyed me*, I thought. I watched it all dissolve in the midst of great loss and grave defeat. As a result of that, I wanted to care, but I knew I could not, and it almost felt as if it became too late for me to do so. My persistence to understand the reasons that everything happened in the past no longer affected me. I thought, *How could it now?* I barely remembered what it was that got me where I stood presently. I thought that vanity and elegance seemed too far away now.

The wind was cold. It got even colder, and the wind blew violently right on my frozen face, while the rest of my body felt as if the cold, violent wind would reach my bones as I walked confidently, watching and observing the reflection of my own shadow. I continued to walk, and I saw a vision that gave me a broken heart filled with bitterness, coldness, darkness, and pain. It felt as if I had drowned my entire childhood in the world of the unknown and the dead. I saw that I had been more of an illusionist than a conscious person. I became upset, tired, and disappointed. I wondered if I had failed everything in life already.

I paused for a while and wondered if it had been the consequence of my mistakes that had failed me, or maybe my own friends, my own family—or was it all the lovers or the lack of prediction of life itself that just failed me and left me really uneasy in a complicated place where no living souls visited? I was in a place as cold as the winter, filled with so much disappointment and regret. The life I once viewed as a way to beauty, love, peace, and every other prestige that followed along with it in every place I went, and in everyone I saw, immediately became very uncertain. I could no longer dream, I ceased watching the sun come up and go down, and my heart began to protest at every opportunity that came my way. And before I could even finish breathing the life out of me, my troubles began. This I saw in my past. It all began when I couldn't answer the simplest question of who I was and what I was to give and to accomplish underneath the existence of my own skin.

My story began when I couldn't tell right from wrong at any cost; I could no longer distinguish the difference between true love from simple infatuation. I started to confound myself with darkness, thinking that maybe I could break all the rules out there and still make it through, with many reproaches to give to God like the one he himself had to give me right where I stood. I became lost and threatened with the idea and image of death that haunted me at night every time I lay down on my cold bed.

I alone was to walk and sort out all this journey; I even tried desiring life to the greatest and the fullest, dreaming of a better life, believing that there was more for me out there. It became both impossible and inevitable, now that every bone inside of me could feel and sense the struggles of my past to the greatest length. I continued my walk, looking straight forward, and I wanted to convince myself to believe that tomorrow could be better. I thought to myself, *If only there could be some sort of charm, magic spell, ritual, or prayer of some kind to rescue me out of this dungeon that I had purposely intruded myself into without realizing it enough on time.*

By now, everyone in my hometown, which is the city of Jacob, already suspected I had gone through a lot, yet I had not realized that despite my perseverance and grand efforts, I was not immortal, nor was I invincible. When I reached a big old tree that no longer had any leaves, I grasped forcefully a memory from the past. I could now see that, as a little girl, every time I found myself in situations that I could not adjust to or deal with, I always took my mind into a world of imagination. There, I tended to find another part of me, another life I managed to create with time. I visualized my life in the shape that I wanted it to be, for as many years as I could remember.

I saw everything in a bright light; I thought my pain was too great to survive the loss I had suffered.

I did, at moments, find myself tortured constantly, night and day, by invisible voices that whispered inside my ears. I thought my journey was not yet completed, that I still had a long journey before me.

While my walk continued, my mind was preoccupied with my past. I saw despair, loneliness, and confusion behind me as if it was ahead of me. At this point, I knew that even my thoughts of hope could not have protected me from the destiny that awaited me. My mind showed me another image of my own past. I saw a quick glimpse of the destiny that I had refused ever since I was a little babe. I remembered refusing to accept that I was just another ordinary girl. I always saw myself as different; I knew from the time that I was seven years old that I was not meant for useless things or unnecessary people. When my mother was still with us, I was very little, weak, truly naïve, and barely aware of what life had in store for me. I recollected my childhood as I walked my way, wrapping my black coat around me even much tighter to protect myself from the wicked cold wind.

Around the age of four, I sat outside the main entrance of my house along with my mother; she said, "You are not just any girl, neither are you just a useless soul; please, always remember, that for me you are the sun that rises in the morning and the star that shines brighter than any other star out there at night."

My recollection of my mother made my palms warm up a little. Mother pampered me with very sweet and tender words; she gazed straight into my eyes and said, "I cherish you profoundly, for you are what I appear to be on the outside, but always remember that inside, you have what I can never have."

I paused my mind forcefully at that memory; I was reluctant to remember more of her. I sighed briefly and continued to force myself with great determination to remember it all. I asked Mother what she meant, and all she did was laugh and reassure me that I would find out on my own someday. I was still a little bit naïve then, but I was reluctant to understand what Maman meant by her piercing words.

The rain started to pour down on me as I continued to walk. I was still in the middle of the park; the wind remained cold, and I was shivering while my teeth chattered against each other. Every drop of rain on my skin felt heavy, while my brain reminded me what my mother once told me. I thought if only if she could see me now from above and see how strange of a woman I had become, I thought that it probably wouldn't be for the best. I had changed completely, I lived in a world of ignorance and extreme insecurity. My paralyzed thoughts of having Mother observe me from above, if ghosts could truly see us, froze my walk for a good ten minutes. I thought, *If only I could go back and be born again and make everything right. somehow.*

I walked speedily to an old abandoned cottage, where I found refuge from the cold rain. I sat quietly, and every memory of the past came to me in a brutal rush, each image having a special detail and meaning of its own. My mother always told me as a little girl that I was a very special soul. She used to tell me that in many forms and many ways, and this much I could still remember.

I became quite accustomed to her story from the day I was born, she reminded me frequently how she nearly died after giving birth to me; to add more to the painful memories, she often mentioned how she struggled during the entire nine months that I was in her womb. She spoke of how poor she and Papa were when they first got married. Still in her painful recollections, she remembered not having many clothes or a decent pair of shoes to go out with; she remembered having nothing to eat for many days because there wasn't enough food for her and my other siblings to eat. She told me how she was not able to go to the hospital in certain time of sickness because of the absence of money.

She told me these things when I was barely eight years old, but I was attentive to her sorrowful life story. I sometimes wondered why she spoke to me about our family's struggles, knowing how incapable I must have felt. I grew up and questioned myself in order to understand it all. I wondered if Mother needed to talk to me about everything our family had gone through simply to remind me that I came from a great struggle, or was it just to teach me to be more like her, strong and brave all at the same time?

After reflecting on those memories, I had a puzzled expression on my face. I asked myself if Mother knew that she would be leaving my siblings and me so soon. At times my recollection of how much my mother had struggled during her entire life, before and after my birth, became a blessing that needed to be honored with great pride and remembrance. On the other hand, it was an eternal curse to be surpassed. The blessing was that in my heart, I always knew that I was her favorite, and the curse was that I strived greatly to please her and make her happy, and for years, I longed for her to heal and get better.

She continued to tell me the story of her life as I grew a little bit older but not necessarily smarter. And so did her chronic illness, which grew even worse. Life at home became more difficult than before. By then I was nearly nine years old, struggling with a sick mother at home every day and every night, wondering in fear what life without a mother would be like.

Months went by fast; I was glad to see that Mother had lived to see me turn nine years old. She was still weak from her illness, but she did find the strength to bake a special birthday cake for me. Mother celebrated my birthday as if she hadn't been ill at all, but she could not deceive me and my siblings for too long. Across the table from where I was sitting, while my entire siblings gathered around the table and the birthday cake to sing me a birthday song, my wide eyes fixed upon Mother's behavior. I watched her condition get much worse.

Mother did not receive a day of rest after my birthday; she became sicker and weaker as each day, week, and month went by. I could no longer hear her tell me a story; it was I who began to tell her plenty of stories, stories that I had personally imagined and invented. Luckily she loved every one of them, and she always asked me to tell her more. I brought her into the magical world of fantasy and illusion; I wanted to make her dream and give her hope that there is always a tomorrow so that she may fight to live long.

One day, I visited her room as she lay on her bed; I took a wooden chair and sat near her bed. She looked into my eyes and asked me if I believed she was going to go to heaven to be with God in case she closed her eyes from this world forever.

When I heard Mother ask me such a question, I halted my attempt to approach her bed so I could be closer to her warm skin. I became upset and troubled by her question; I thought she was being very selfish as a mother. I thought she was not thinking of what was to become of me, her daughter, plus her other children after she was gone. I wondered how we were going to cope or even survive if she ever left us.

I pulled myself away, not feeling any sympathy for her; instead, I felt profuse anger—even though I knew just how ill and weak she was. The room got cold; Mother was too weak to dry the tears that were falling from my eyes.

She said very softly, in a pleading voice, "Please, do not cry."

I ignored her plea, seeking even greater attention while I counted under my breath her every bone and compared them to that of a child—so thin, so weak, and so soft.

I stood up as the rain ceased to fall. I looked back from where I began my walk, to see how far I had come so far, and I continued my memories' evaluation. I felt that Mother and I had both been very selfish human beings. Mother only thought about her departure from earth to heaven, I thought, and not us. She was not reluctant to leave this world, including her children. She wanted desperately to leave everything behind her, even though we needed her. I sighed, and my heart felt heavy.

I continued to allow my mind to travel back to the past whenever I felt the urge to do so. I thought about my own survival; I thought about my own life, my destiny, and what it would become now that everything appeared to be so clear. I remembered walking out of Mother's room, inconsolable. I went to the nearest tree and sat there quietly, lost in thoughts. The thought of being without a mother haunted my mind endlessly. Growing up in the city of Jacob, I had seen how harshly and cruelly people could treat children without a mother. All the hope I had stored in my heart for a happy life, I felt, was snatched brutally away from me, and all the dreams I had were gone. I no longer believed in the stories that I grew up hearing, and I no longer told these stories to my comrades.

I sat beneath the shade tree for more than an hour, feeling all the frustration that the day had to offer. I went inside to a cold, dark room that was once used by my grandmother, Papa's mother. She spent her time inside the room when she had been ill before she passed away. I needed to visit Grandmother's room again; I needed to feel something. I felt certain that life was treating me unfairly, things seemed to take a bad turn on me, and it appeared as if everyone around me seemed to challenge me. I took my shoes off when I entered the room, I wanted my feet to feel the cold floor; everything was covered with dust, even the bed where Grandmother once laid upon looked dusty, for the room had not been used in years. I knelt down on my knees for hours, hoping that I would hear God's voice respond to my prayer. Still bending down on my knees, I waited to hear God speak to me until I fell asleep.

The next morning, I woke up with my knees hurting, only to hear from Aunt Ursula, my father's distant cousin, that Mother had departed from this world. She said it with a firm voice. She continued, without any expression of remorse, "Your mother no longer breathes and walks among us; she is gone, she is now in heaven singing and interceding for us with all the angels and the saints."

At that moment, I could no longer hear or feel anything, my mouth refused to say a single word despite every effort I strived to make, my entire body refused to obey me when I obliged it to move, my muscles ached as if a train had just passed over me, tears flowed out of my eyes, everything at that particular time hurt without explanation. I took off from where I was, and I knew just how well darkness surrounded my mind as I wondered what I needed to do next. I wanted to just die. I thought that if I took my own life, no one would ever forgive me, nor would God. So I stood in one place for as long as I could; there, I continued to be lost in my dark thoughts. My heart felt as cold as the heart of a king.

I became exhausted with not only my own struggles but that of my brothers and my sister, Julie. Julie was the oldest of us all, and by the time our mother died, she was already turning nineteen. Julie found herself lost in all that was happening around her, and I was feeling so depressed and deserted by the cruelty of people and the reality of life itself, that she did not find my ability to console her reliable, and so she found comfort in the arms of her first love, Arnold, a boy our mother detested. Before she had died, Mother forbade Julie from seeing Arnold.

I remembered vividly every word my mother used to tell Julie about Arnold; she would say, "Arnold is up to no good; he will only use you and then coldly discard you after all is said and done."

But I don't believe Julie ever took that advice seriously until a little while after our mother's burial. We left Jacob to take Mother's body to Le Bleue for burial in the nearby town of Joie d'Olive. Julie's closest friend, Sara, arrived from Jacob to express in person her profound sympathy toward us of our mother's death. Several days after her arrival, she sat down with Julie in the kitchen, reassuring her that what she was about to tell her came from a truthful source and that she did not want to see her suffer or break her heart. As Sara spoke to Julie, I was at the corner, watching them both.

Sara's face got very tense, her eyes directed only toward Julie, and then she said, "Julie, I have some bad news for you concerning Arnold." She continued while I watched their conversation attentively. "Arnold has found himself not only one girl to flirt with but several of them, ever since you left Jacob to come here for your mother's burial."

I continued to watch them both speak; as they whispered, I became less concerned with what Sara was telling Julie, and more concerned with the pain, confusion, and humiliation that were now visible on Julie's face. I had thought to observe their conversation to entertain my mind, but it had turned into sadness. I knew too well how madly and passionately in love she had been with Arnold. I thought, *Does he not have a heart or the least bit of common sense, for him to betray her just a few weeks after their separation?*

I was certainly crushed, and my little hope of ever finding that one true love that everybody dreams about was crushed as well. I asked myself if love was even worth the search and the wait. I turned pale when Julie approached me to tell me what Arnold had done.

With tears in her eyes, she cried out, "Judette, Arnold has betrayed me after I have given him all my love and trust. Mother warned me about this, but I failed to listen to her. How sorry I am now." She continued, "Now I am all confused, unable to understand why he betrayed me."

She sighed miserably while she complained to me about Arnold. I reached out and laid my hand on her shoulder, reassuring her that it was indeed Arnold's loss and not hers. She stared at me with a very frank gaze and then replied, "In time, I should forget all about him," and I said, "You sure will."

Meanwhile, on my part, months went by without any kind of consolation to appease my heart whatsoever. In my case, the idea that time heals all wounds was proved a lie. I still can't imagine this being true. We had moved to the city of Le Bleue, close to where our mother was buried in Joie d'Olive. The town peasants stared at me strangely as the new girl in town. They knew that I had come from another city, a city well known for its grand festivals. As much as I tried to make myself believe that Le Bleue was not all that bad, I still could not shake myself out of my many nightmares, no matter what I did.

I became extremely distant from it all, especially from life itself. I began to walk the streets of Le Bleue as much as I could; it was the only thing that kept my mind preoccupied and disconnected from my true feelings and all that surrounded me. When I reached my tenth birthday, no one noticed or even cared to throw me any kind of party such as the ones I was accustomed to when Mother was still alive. There was no nice cake like the ones Mother used to bake for special celebrations, there was not even the simplest gift to cheer me up, and there were no birthday cards filled with words of gentleness and tenderness like the ones Mother used to write to me on my birthday.

No one at the house noticed that it was my birthday; rather than to protest from the cold treatment, I felt relieved that no one had remembered at all, since this would be my first celebration without Mother.

About a year after moving to Le Bleue, everything in me faded as each day went by; I wanted nothing to do with my school, I spent most of my time with my new friends. I found them very unusual; they were thin, with pale skin, and very tall in height. These girls were as strong as men, and they spent most of their days working under the sun, cultivating all types of plants, vegetables, and fruits. Sometimes they would go fishing and I would just lie down on the green grass in astonishment, thinking to myself how strong and brave these young girls truly were. They didn't spend much time at all looking in the mirror, and they did not care about what kind of makeup they had on, nor did they care about the shoes or dresses they had on either. I can't remember any of these girls wearing any type of makeup, powder, lipstick, or perfume. I asked myself if they had little time for it, or if there was a chance that they didn't think things like makeup existed out there.

After living in Le Bleue for about a year, I became exhausted with the way the people lived their lives. I went through a phase of depression and hopelessness for many months, but I observed my brothers and sister adjust pretty easily and amicably with everyone. Another year later, Papa traveled to another city, and his departure pleased me very much, because for many years Papa had dreamed of traveling , and he had spoken of this dream to everyone he knew, ever since I was still a little child. I felt at least he was lucky enough to fly far away from all the suffering and death that was happening in the family.

A couple of months after Papa left for the city of Lacote, we learned that my mother's mother had been hit and killed by a train; this news saddened me, but I was too weak to grieve her properly, and I became much too detached from people, events, relations, and places. Death in my family continued to touch and ravage those it touched. We then learned that my mother's brother, who had lived in Le Bleue during his whole life, had died from an unknown disease. I began to feel that maybe the departed were better off in heaven, assisting my mother and reassuring her that we were all right, letting her know that she need not worry, wherever she was. I began to wonder if in some mysterious ways she was able to watch me, see me, protect me, and console me without my knowledge.

One night, I sat down outside not too far from her grave; I could see just how bright each star shined, I gazed directly at each one of them; I recalled what my mother used to tell me, that I was everything she was in the outside yet in the inside having all the greatness that she could never have.

I thought, *All right, I get it, I get it all now, and it's all coming into one place.* I began to see it all in a new perspective; I could also see what wasn't there before. I thought maybe if I tried harder, as Mother used to do, all the pieces will surely connect to its own rightful place; at least that's what I told myself then, not knowing that there was more to it than what I imagined there to be.

While I was trying to be this new brave girl that would no longer be afraid or spend her days in tears grieving her mother, I discovered a new passion, and that passion was to go to church as often as possible. When I began my search for the light, which I referred to as my search for the truth, I became amused that there was actually a different world out there that I hadn't known at all. People filled my curiosity; I became aware that there were groups that were perfected and not at all afflicted, like the ones I was used to being around. The perfected ones believed that there were answers and explanations to every loss, suffering, pain, defeat, and death. And the afflicted were those who suffered and did not understand the cause behind those sufferings.

I began my initiation at the age of eleven. I joined a religious group called the La Fontaine. I attended this particular group filled with perfected men and women for one year. I believed at the time that it would bring me healing, harmony, and peace from all the darkness that surrounded me after my mother's death. And so a new journey began for me. I attended La Fontaine three to four times a week. On Mondays, I took singing lessons; on Tuesdays, I took meditation lessons; on Thursdays, we all studied; on Fridays, one of the men from La Fontaine came to my home and gave me singing lessons. I took all these activities very seriously; I can still remember some of the songs they used to sing at La Fontaine.

While I was making a new discovery into a new and different world, my brothers constantly made fun of me; they couldn't believe that I, who was very well known for my moodiness, began to conduct myself with a very positive attitude toward life. I continued my attendance at La Fontaine; Papa heard of my new path from my brothers; they told Papa how I had changed and how I had become a much happier person compared to before. He then sent me a new dress to congratulate me on my new path in life. He ordered it straight from the city of Jacob, and it meant the world to me for Papa to encourage me.

One of the brothers from La Fontaine always came to our home to give me voice lessons; his name was Frère Martin, but unfortunately that didn't work too well. As much as I wanted to sing in the choir, he bluntly informed me that God had not blessed me with a beautiful voice; of course I knew he spoke only the truth but that didn't stop my feelings from being hurt. I was covered with embarrassment and disappointment after he had told me that I could not sing at all.

Afterward, Frère Martin suggested that I learn how to dance, but since I was still embarrassed by his remarks about how poorly I sang, I ceased from going regularly to La Fontaine. I was discouraged from the truth; I wanted to sing so much that I couldn't recover from the cold truth that he had revealed to me. Now that I look back, I think to myself, *Poor man, I resented him for telling me what I actually couldn't do.*

Season after season, I began to get used to living in Le Bleue. Life still wasn't easy, but I thought to myself that I either had to make the best out of where I was or live miserably for the rest of my life. On the other hand, Papa was enjoying his new life as the ambassador to Lacote. Papa constantly sent us beautiful letters and pictures; from the look of his photos, I could visualize every word he had written in his letters. He described Lacote as a paradise.

I was very happy for Papa, but I felt that it should have been me (and perhaps all of my siblings) walking side by side down the streets of Lacote with Papa, discussing politics and going to tea party after tea party, but mostly I wanted to feel the touch of the sand, which he walked upon in all of his photos. I took one of his photos he had sent us and hid it under my pillows, and I imagined that someday I would also be walking the streets of Lacote with Papa.

By now my sister Julie had gotten herself a new boyfriend; his name was Robert Charles. I wasn't very fond of him at all, and I always thought his brother was much more handsome than he was. Robert was about six feet, six inches tall, while Julie was only five feet, five inches. I found their union much too strange to understand. The sun had made his skin as dark as the evening of fall. His face was not at all flattering; it always looked as if he was really exhausted and he needed to rest. I wondered sometimes if Arnold's betrayal of her love had been why she could not pick the right guy for her; had she become that insecure? So insecure that she would date someone out of her league?

Of course, I kept these questions to myself, as well as my feelings about how ugly I thought Robert was. I knew I could never tell her that her second boyfriend was a poor choice, but to my relief, he was very much in love with her. He cherished her, he respected her very much, and he made her feel like a princess, which I always knew she was because of her great beauty, which was as radiant as fresh white roses of spring. None of the other girls in Le Bleue could compare to her. I believed at the time that everyone was just as shocked as I was when she picked Robert as her new boyfriend; she could have done so much better, since she had so many handsome guys who were dying to date her, perhaps even marry her. While Julie returned to the dating field, I was just glad to see her smile again, even though Robert wasn't as handsome as Arnold.

Meanwhile, my brothers were really busy with their own lives; they were adjusting quicker and easier than I was. Growing up with many brothers and only one sister was at times challenging to the mind and the soul. Julie was the oldest of us all, Mark was the eldest boy, after Mark came Jacque, then Justin; after Justin, I came, then Mathieu, then came the twins Laurent and Laurence, and last came Leon. Having so many siblings was often exhausting because there came a time when watching them became unbearable. I remember complaining about why Papa and Maman had so many of us, especially now that Mother was no longer with us.

Of course, there were days when we all enjoyed each other's company, especially during the cold weather, when we all sat gladly around the fire, telling each other stories about how great it had been when Maman had been around, and how her stories were always filled with words of hope and magic, which brought great comfort and love in each single one of our hearts. Maman was no longer with us, and Papa often traveled, which meant we were left to take care of one another. As for Julie, she was very good at making sure that Leon's needs were well met.

I, on the other hand, was too busy thinking of my own happiness; I ventured around the bushes, catching beautiful butterflies in all types of colors, imprisoning them inside my little bottle. It never occurred to me then that these butterflies wanted as much freedom as I did. I always saw the world as a place of entanglement, and at the same time I found myself entangling others in each way that I could. After a couple of months, I became bored with going to the woods to catch beautiful butterflies. I began to think that maybe I could do more work like the work other young girls in our new city were doing. So I went down to Joie d'Olive, the town where my mother was buried. It had been more than two years, and still I could feel a little chill while I passed by the street of St. Joseph, just a couple of blocks away from Maman's grave.

I passed the street of St. Joseph in a hurry; a feeling of paranoia filled my veins, and I became as cold as the morning air. I had taken off my shoes to run down that street as fast as I could, but my gut was telling me not to run. I ignored that feeling and began to run. I found myself on an unknown street where a couple of girls were swimming in a small lake. They looked like they could have been between twelve and fourteen, so I asked them, as friendly as I could, if I could join them. At the time, I felt if only I could swim as much as I could, then I could gain two new friends, someone to walk the street of St. Joseph with, perhaps someone to help me get to whatever destination my path was leading me at that moment.

I made this request, and they gladly agreed; they said at once, "Please, do feel free to join us, for it is our pleasure to swim with a new friend."

I was very much flattered by their warm acceptance. I took off my blue sleeveless dress, which I had worn on that hot sunny day, and I looked at them in the eyes. I remember making such a powerful jump into the water, and the next thing I knew, I was being rescued by two gentlemen that the girls had cried out to, as I flailed in the water because I did not know how to swim.

When I returned to the world of consciousness, I could hear loud voices, and I could barely remember what had just happened. I asked the two gentlemen why they had to hold me in each one of their arms; what had happened to me? Over and over again, I asked the men this question.

They stared into each other's eyes, puzzled, which began to scare me, then one of the two gentlemen answered, "Well, you almost drowned, Mademoiselle."

After he said that, I tried to pull myself up and be still all at one time; the other gentleman, who wore tight, old-fashioned black shorts and no shirt, helped me to carefully sit up. While the two girls I had just met stared at me with fear, I began to walk away as quickly as I could. I had barely gained my strength back and struggled to move from one place to the next.

I thanked both men without even bothering to ask for their names, and then I sped away as fast as I could, like the wind itself. At the same time, I gave the girls a look of terror. I suspected they had used black magic on me to drown me in the deep, cold water, since they could tell by my manners that I was not from the city of Le Bleue. I was as stunned as they were; while I walked past them, I thought how my life could have ended there, without my brothers' and sister's knowledge of what had happened to me.

My plan to become more active now vanished, and I became lost again without a plan. I felt as cold as the dry winter while I walked back home. I started to wonder if maybe there was a certain spell or evil force out there trying to get me, just like it had gotten my mother. Although I had heard mysterious stories about Le Bleue, which was very well known for its practice of both black magic and witchcraft, I tended to ignore them all. For me those stories were just silly myths that people told in order to make life even harder for anyone who was not from Le Bleue.

As I walked home down the street of St. Joseph, I murmured softly to myself, "someone please come to my rescue." After repeating this several times, I paused for a second to wonder if I had become like one of those people who lived their lives in doubt of good, fearing that there could be evil forces out there, just waiting to trap them. These thoughts traveled my mind, and I became paralyzed like a dead body. I whispered to myself that if only I had asked those two gentlemen who had helped me out of the water to escort me home, they would have felt some sort of pity for me and would have taken me home. I would have been home by now.

While I walked quickly, I thought of my brothers (and my sister Julie, of course), wondering if they had become worried about my absence since it was getting really dark. The sky was as dark as midnight without any moon to give it the beauty of light. I reached a nearby crossroad and saw a bridge; it looked none too pleasing. The bridge reminded me of the story Maman used to tell me, the story of the king who ruled the dead. The bridge curved down to its right as if to reach the dark water, and as I observed this bridge, my skin shivered and I began to tremble. I murmured to myself, wondering if this was just another punishment from God since I had spoken of death several times. I wondered if God was trying to grant me my wish of dying, or was it just witchcraft thrown at me by the people of Le Bleue?

I stood before the dark, scary bridge, telling myself that there was no way I was going to cross it. I began to return to the lake where I had almost drowned, hoping to find the two gentlemen who had saved me. At that point, I felt really uneasy, with nothing and no one at all to console me. I wondered how to get out of the situation I was in; I thought, *What a nightmare!*

I walked back to the lake; by this time I could feel the terrible cold wind making my soft, sensitive skin shiver. The darkness and fear controlled my mind and took possession of my body and sense of reality. I started to recall all the tales and stories Mother used to tell me as a little girl. One of the stories was my mother's favorite; she always gathered all of my brothers and sister to tell the story of **Nadia**, a girl who was ten years old. Her stepmother, named Lily, used to have a habit of sending her alone to the river to fetch some water to be used at home. Her stepmother, who clearly was an evil witch, saw this as an opportunity to both punish Nadia and put her in great danger.

Nadia was usually obedient, but one day she felt the need to refuse to obey her stepmother, because she did not feel well. When Nadia refused to obey her stepmother's demand, Lily forcefully pushed her out the door, telling her not to return home until she had fetched enough water in order to cook and clean the floor.

Little Nadia, as sick as she felt that day, left home and went to the river, except this time she didn't walk as fast as she usually did; before she knew it, the sun went down on her so fast that it became both cold and dark. She started to cry, with no one to come to her rescue; she reached the river and started to fetch the water.

After she finished fetching the water, the river became as dark as a winter night, trees started to whisper, there was a very strong wind, frogs sang from all over the river, and all the stars in the sky were covered by a really dark cloud. She suddenly heard the deep voice of a man calling her name; she turned around to see who was there in the middle of the forest with no one else except herself (well, at least that's what she thought).

As she turned around, fear crawled beneath her skin, and she saw no one at all. She began to hurry away from the river, presuming that her fear had made her mind imagine that someone had called her name. As she tried to walk away from the river, she once again heard a loud voice, and this time it was as strong as the sound of thunder.

The night grew even darker and the wind became both loud and violent; she took off her sandals with thoughts of running away from the voices, but she sensed that wouldn't do her any good at all, so she responded with a reserved tone, "Who are you and what do you want, or should I say, what do you want from me?"

The voice replied, "I am the spirit who guards this river, and I am not too pleased with anyone who touches my river when the sky turns dark."

Nadia, with a trembling voice, cried out, "It was not from my own will that I have come to fetch water so late, rather it was my stepmother's wish that I do so."

The spirit of the river stood before little Nadia as tall as a palm tree; he approached Nadia as she begged for her life, and then the spirit of the river made a proposal that Nadia should have refused.

The spirit of the water told her, "I will let you return freely to your home, but in return, I want only one wish that I desire greatly, and that wish is for me to have you as my wife."

Nadia replied to the spirit of the river, "Please, spare me and let me go back home. I will do as you please and marry you; I will become your wife if only you spare me this night and allow me to return back home."

The spirit of the river replied, "Very well," and allowed Nadia to return to her home in the village; she kept the story of what happened from both her father and stepmother.

Years went by. Little Nadia forgot the promise she had made to the spirit of the river, and one night as she was preparing to say her prayers and go to bed, she heard the loud deep voice of the spirit of the river. When she tried to see who had called her name, Nadia turned into a bowl of water. As my mother told us the story, the people of Le Bleue believed that it was indeed Nadia's stepmother who sent the spirit of the river to scare little Nadia and trick her into signing for her own death. My mother never quite finished the story of what happened to little Nadia and her evil stepmother.

I thought about all the stories that Maman had told me as a little girl; I couldn't help but feel like little Nadia at this point. I walked straight without turning back, telling myself that turning back would be a huge mistake; that was the mistake that little Nadia made, turning back, I thought.

After walking about thirty minutes, I grew exhausted and started to hear laughter, only to find that those voices belonged to Julie and her new boyfriend, Robert. I cried aloud, exclaiming how glad I was to see them both. They gazed at me with curiosity and asked where I had been; the two of them had been looking for me for the past two hours, they said, with no success whatsoever.

I paused for a minute and said, "Well, Julie, you seem to be enjoying your time more than you were looking for me," and it was very clear that Julie was having more fun than I had expected. When I discovered them, Robert was holding her left hand while she stared deeply into his eyes.

Julie was embarrassed by my blunt comment and blushed as she proceeded to tell me that Papa had written each of us a special letter, and my letter was at home, on my bed, waiting for me. It was definitely the best news I had had for a long time. Then I told Julie to ask Robert to stop being so flirtatious and take us home as quickly as possible.

Julie replied, with an irritable tone, "Fine, we shall go," as she kissed Robert very passionately good-bye on the cheek; they both blushed, avoiding my eyes, afraid that I may look at them with both fury and disgust.

We left the street of St. Joseph and went home; I told myself what a day that had been and not just any day but a cursed one, which could have ended terribly if Julie and Robert had not caught up with me. I was finally at home, and Julie wondered what had happened to me that evening. I walked among my brothers, wished them well, and told them how pleased I was to see them and to be by their sides.

A few minutes after my parade of joy and laughter, Julie caught me by surprise and snatched me away from all my brothers. She wanted to talk to me in private, and she said I must promise to never tell a soul as long as I lived. She had a very serious tone as she told me that she needed to share something with me and that it was very urgent that I learn about it; she would have approached me earlier, if only she had gotten the chance to do so.

She took both my hands, bent down, and whispered very softly in my ears, "I am in love."

I thought, *Oh, well, weren't you in love with Arnold too?* Hadn't she learned anything concerning men, especially with what Arnold did to her just after Mother died? As she whispered those words to me, I glanced at her face; I could see her disappointment since I had not reacted as she thought I would. I faked a smile and reassured her that I was very pleased to learn that she had found herself a new love interest, and that her secret was to remain safe with me.

I jumped on my bed and opened the letter Papa had sent me; this was my only consolation at the moment. My joy of being saved had been crushed by my sister's feelings for Robert, and I wanted to fly away and never again return; then I thought about my experience and all the things that I had gone through that day; I could only thank God for making it home safely.

Time went by fast, and I grew to detest it all, all over again. I became more unhappy with everything, I still had thoughts of running away, I remembered feeling as cold as the morning water yet managing to smile, and the more I pretended to smile and to be as happy as one could be, the worse I felt inside. I became insecure at the idea of not fitting in at all. I detested the way the people of Le Bleue lived their lives so carelessly; at times I wondered what I was doing in their city. I went to church without hope and got back from church ceremonies without faith. I couldn't understand why there was so much suffering in Le Bleue; why couldn't everyone just find their ways and become happier?

As each day passed, I had many questions that circulated within my mind. I frequently questioned my existence, why I was here, and why couldn't I just be happy; those questions were not answered; in fact, they were never answered by Papa or by the priest. I became more and more lost in my own mind; I began to confound deceptions with illusions, and the period of emptiness and confusion surrendered my heart.

I began to bask in the memories of my past. I remembered as a little girl being very stubborn; I had the courage to fight all the boys my age and took great pride in doing so. I played ball with the boys in my neighborhood; I was determined to prove that girls were just as active, strong, and brave as the boys. In the long run it paid off, boys in my neighborhood started to invite me more often to play on behalf of their team, and I always felt flattered by this offer, but not everyone liked this. Madame Rosen, who lived just a block from where I lived, was always aggravated whenever she watched me kick the ball.

At the time, it was very much prohibited by any city for girls to play ball, so it always made Madame Rosen very displeased to see me kicking the ball. She always shouted at me, "Shame on you, young girl, and your mother should be blamed for all this."

This always used to irritate me, and I never enjoyed her presence, just as she did not enjoy mine. I hated when she stared at me with her eyes, which were easily mistaken for those of a viper, both vicious and cold. I hated her constant remarks on how I should act like a lady because I was a lady; I hated even the sound of her voice alone.

I was relieved when Theresa, one of my closest friends, told me that Madame Rosen had moved away. I could never wish ill matters on anyone, but at the same time I couldn't resist celebrating her departure. I felt free, free to play ball as much as I wanted. My joy for playing ball didn't last long; by the time summer ended, I had discovered a new passion, hiking to the top of the mountains, smelling the fresh air as the wind blew in my face, screaming loud as I could to hear my own voice echo back to me very loudly. I also continued to collect all types of butterflies, in all sort of colors, blue, brown, white, golden, and they were always cheerful to touch and to watch.

But no matter how hard I tried to preoccupy my mind from the pain, emptiness, and distress, nothing seem to console me, not even on Friday mornings when I would confess to Father Jean about my inner trouble. My actions ceased to carry the passion and enthusiasm they once did, my moods became as divers as that of a lost child, I began to lose weight as time passed, for I had ceased to eat as often as I should.

This solitude lasted nearly three years until I met Karla, who was my age; she was the daughter of one of the great chiefs in the city of Le Bleue. The opinion of her family was very much respected, for they were rich in every way one could think of. Her father, Monsieur Maurice, owned houses, and farms in every corner of Le Bleue. Her mother owned restaurants she had inherited from her late father, who had raised her on his own.

Despite Karla's great family wealth, she comforted me in her sincerity and friendship. Karla was warm, kind, honest, and generous; she never boasted about her family's wealth. She always was kind to all, whether they were rich or poor. She spent most of her days with me when she wasn't helping her mother at the restaurant.

Karla became my true and only friend. I could confide in her about my feelings, my fears, and my deepest dreams, and she always told me how well she understood the pain inside of me and prayed that I could find great comfort in her mother instead of dwelling in the past. My desire to die or run away from home became less as Karla filled my days with great stories, and adventures, and beautiful dreams. She and I always went to the most isolated parts of the city; we ran and screamed as if we were free from it all, we pretended to be royalty, which always added more to our pride since she and I believed that a lady should only be treated with the most tender manners that a princess or a queen received.

During the entire time that I spent with Karla, I felt an escape from my mental discontentment. It became clear that I had finally found my lost self, a new hope to live and a new best friend in Karla, and I thought that nothing could possibly go wrong. At least that's what I thought until I heard that Karla was being sent away to study art at a great school, which she had always wanted to do. After I learned the sad news about Karla's departure, I became ill from it all, and Karla must have learned of my illness from Julie, because I received a basket of fruit from Karla with a card saying, "Get well, for you are my one and only friend and I will not leave for school until I learn you are well."

Tears dropped softly on my cheek as I read the card. I was touched by Karla's gesture of sympathy, kindness, and care, and I decided to force myself up and go to Karla's house. When Julie saw me out of the bed, she protested with a concerned voice, telling me I needed more rest and saying that Karla would surely understand.

Ignoring my sister's advice, I grabbed an apple from the basket and struggled to put on my pink dress with violet flowers; suddenly, I heard a knock on the door, and the next thing I heard was Karla's voice. I sat on my bed, at once feeling relief that I no longer needed to go to her, instead she came to me, and before I even got the chance to call her, she entered my room with Julie at her side. She bent down, hugged me, and gently touched my right hand. She paused for a minute, gazing at my wrist.

She whispered, "You need to get well, not only for your own sake but also for mine."

I smiled softly and replied, "I will, Karla; it's just a matter of seconds and you shall see me again back on my two feet."

But a week later, my fever became worse as my headaches increased. I grabbed my pillow every night to recite prayers before I went to bed. Julie grew worried about this and decided that I was to consult a physician; her suggestion was immediately followed the next day. When Julie and I arrived at the hospital, doctors were rushed to my side for I was too ill for them to wait. From the moment I reached the hospital, I could not recollect anything that had happened the previous day.

I woke up the next day in a very cold room, feeling better but exhausted, and I barely gained more of my consciousness. Around my bed, I perceived Karla and all my brothers; Julie was talking to the doctor. Karla touched my forehead and asked if I was all right; I replied, "I'll live."

My brother Mathieu suggested I needed a drink of water, but I refused to drink anything. Leon then spoke, sounding more concerned than ever. He said, "You know you're going to kill yourself before death finds you, you cannot starve yourself forever, neither should you deprive yourself of water."

Karla turned to Leon and touched his shoulder, reassuring him that she would make sure that I ate and drank before she left the hospital. My days at the hospital went smoothly. Doctor Leblanc took very good care of me; he made sure that I consumed enough food and drink to gain my strength quickly. I had wasted so much energy and had lost a lot of weight at the time. I rested as much as possible, and each time the nurse came to give me medication, he was always there at my side, encouraging me to take my medicine so that I could recover quickly.

On my last day at the hospital, he hugged me, kissing me on the cheek and telling me to call him if I needed anything. Doctor Leblanc's kindness was a greater remedy than the medications that I took. After I got out of the hospital, I began to regain my health and strength back, but I couldn't avoid the reality that Karla would soon be leaving Le Bleue to go to La Piege, where she was to study arts. I knew this day would come, and my heart was filled with great sadness.

It was unbearable to watch her packing. I could barely breathe and I choked at each single thought that reminded me of how awful life was to become without her, at my side, as a friend. While I faced the moment of despair, tears dropped from Karla's eyes. I ran to her side and held her hand in mine; we both hugged each other as if we were never going to part and again broke down into tears until no more tears could be shed.

She promised to write to me as soon as she got to La Piege, but little did we both know that we were never going to see each other again. She looked as radiant as the morning sun as she left Le Bleue for La Piege. Her bright yellow dress made her light brown eyes sparkle, and I told her how beautiful she looked.

A month after Karla left Le Bleue, I was alone and bored again. I contemplated myself throughout long distance walks, I went from one place to another, looking for meaningful dreams and new ideas, since my own no longer appeased me. At times, I wrote down my dreams of traveling to far-off places but found myself at once burning those dreams. I found them unachievable, unnecessary at times, and useless to others.

My distress grew and so did my fear. I wanted nothing of the world, and I felt the same way every day; no change came to me, nothing seemed to impress me. I was very much lost, and as lost as I was, I found that a part of me longed to be lost purposely at times; it was my way of vanishing from all sort of pains and sufferings. After Karla left, she didn't write to me at all, as she had promised, neither did I hear anything from her, and her silence only added boredom and distress to my heart.

For many months, I watched our friendship vanish from her absence; a couple more months went by, and I no longer missed Karla, rather I found myself upset at her for betraying our friendship with false promises and a cold silence. I told myself, *A few more years will fix all this; I'll probably end up somewhere doing great things with my dreams.*

One morning, I woke up thinking of my aunt, my mother's older sister; her name was Gisela. Tante Gisela (Aunt Gisela) was very slim and tall; she had in her the strength of a lion. Growing up, I had heard only great stories involving her and wonderful things about her; she was married at one point in her life, but each time she had a child, the child never reached a month or two. By the time she and her husband reached their tenth anniversary, she had lost and buried six children, and her husband's family had threatened to find him another wife, which they later on did, and her husband, believing that she was actually a sorceress, abandoned her with no words of explanation whatsoever.

She remarried to a science teacher; with the grace of God on her side, she got pregnant, gave birth to a son, and named him Victoir, meaning victory. The child fortunately lived, he was now my age. Many thoughts of her penetrated my mind; I suddenly felt the urge to visit her, thinking maybe her resemblance to Maman would fulfill my heart.

I ran inside and impatiently searched for my favorite shoes. I found them underneath my brown schoolbag and abruptly grabbed them; I thought about praying to keep certain evil forces away from my soul. I grabbed my green sweater from my bed. I set out with both joy and excitement for my trip to Tante Gisela's house. Although I'd seen her at Maman's funeral, I had not seen her at all after the funeral, and I thought to myself, *Why hadn't I thought about her much sooner? When I felt lonely and afraid, why didn't I run to her warm embrace, hugs and kisses, for both comfort and clarity when I had felt so alone and lost for so many months?*

I walked down the street of St. Peter while these questions encircled my mind; not too attached to the subject, I found myself wondering the true cause behind Karla's silence. It made no sense at all; it wasn't her style to be inconsiderate of other people's feelings. I thought, *Hadn't she missed me at all? Did she get to the city of La Piege safely? If so what prevented her from writing to me even a single sentence of her wellness, and what she liked or disliked about the city?*

I was so lost in my own thoughts, I nearly forgot to turn right onto St. Laurence Avenue. My body became possessed with anxiety as I approached Tante Gisela's house, for I hadn't seen her for nearly four years, and the last time I had seen her it was at the funeral. She and I didn't have much time to get acquainted very well, but she did introduce herself to us. She spoke in a very loving tone, telling us that she was indeed Maman's older sister, which made her our close and direct aunt by blood.

I finally got to where she lived. I approached her yard carefully, not wanting to create any scene, but deep inside I wished to do just that. To my surprise, her reaction to me was both quick and accurate. She turned around, opening her mouth widely, with tears of both joy and sadness in her eyes, crying out my name, "Judette! Judette! Judette, oh my dear Judette, is it truly you or am I dreaming for the moment?"

I was so flattered by her joy to have me at her home, I released out of my heart all the doubts and anxiety that I had carried with me on the way to her house. Next she touched my face with tears flowing from her deep, dark, piercing eyes.

She said, "Your beautiful face is just like that of your mother, Marie, and if only she was here to see the beautiful young version of herself that you have grown to be." She murmured to herself, "Thanks be to God, for this miracle, which is nothing but a piece of Marie herself that she has left behind for us to witness."

I basked in pride and dignity as she compared my face and beauty to Maman's. I couldn't wish for any other look except of that of my mother. But then again, why was I so sad? I was now at Tante Gisela's house; the least I could do was appease my wondering mind of the past's loss and enjoy her most vibrant presence. Seeing Tante Gisela reminded me so much of Maman; we found ourselves being reminded of how things were and how easy and wonderful life had been then, when we could feel and touch her with love, passions, and dreams.

Now it all seemed to fade away in the glimpse of Mother's departure. Tante Gisela proposed that I sit down, since I had been on the road for quite a while. I gladly accepted her offer, and so I sat, while she went back inside her house only to bring out an old rugged photo album made of brown leather. You could tell that the album had been with her for ages. She handed me the photo album while she fixed us some herbal tea. I sneezed a lot; the photo album was covered with lots of dust. It appeared to me that the photo album had not been glanced at or even touched in many years.

Tante Gisela approached me with two cups of hot tea, she gave me mine, taking a seat close to my chair. The wind outside was not blowing as hard as it usually does during the month of September; rather, the trees surrounding her house sat still, not dropping as many leaves as that of my neighbor's house. A few minutes after she took her seat, she slowly grabbed the photo album from me, and the first page she opened was two little girls, about seven years old, in pink dresses and carrying roses.

I asked who the two young girls were; she responded with a breaking voice, which sounded as soft as that of newborn baby, "It is your mother and I, we were both coming from the church. We had just witnessed the christening of Gabriel, your uncle, who was just a month old."

She moved to the next page, ignoring the next photo, which showed a tall man with long braided hair, dressed all in white. Continuing to discuss the subject of Gabriel, she said, "He is your uncle; don't ever forget that. Although he was not as close to your mother as he is to me, do not allow any doubts to deprive you of your uncle's love and wealth as long as you live." She gazed at the sun and continued, "He may drink a lot, but that doesn't mean he is unaware of the agony Marie's death has caused our family to suffer. So remember, my dear child, never allow any stories that you hear of your uncle Gabriel to destroy your right to his love and wealth."

She turned to the next page, even though she had not explained who the tall man was. I observed her attentively; the intensity in her face increased when she reached the third page of the album.

She sighed, saying, "This is your great-grand-tante Françoise; she was a mysterious woman. She came to the city of Jacob at the age of seventeen; she had run away from her uncle, who turned her into his mistress, breaking the promise he had made to her parents that he would take care of her. Françoise came to Jacob with no acquaintances, no knowledge of the language, no place to stay during the cold, dangerous nights.

"She developed her talents for agriculture to feed herself; she also earned enough to buy new dresses, for it was very much required then for a lady to look both proper and very well dressed. One rainy day after church, she met Olivier, who introduced her to your great-grand-uncle Jonathan."

Tante Gisela released some of her facial distress by taking a very deep breath. "Your great-grand-tante and great-grand-uncle married two years after they met; they married in accordance with their faith, and they both took great pride in being true-born children of God. For seven years of marriage, your great-grand-tante Françoise tried to have kids without any success; too consumed with both pain and humiliation, she suggested that Jonathan take another wife so that he would not be deprived of having children.

"He rejected her proposal furiously, but he later agreed to the idea, in order to appease Françoise's broken heart. He married a much younger woman; her name was Claudette, and she came from the city of Drolline, where cows and sheep were often raised. She was very beautiful; everyone noticed her beauty the minute she arrived in the city of Jacob. Your great-grand-tante Françoise took a quick liking to her, and she always told Claudette that she was like the little sister she never had.

"Unfortunately, Claudette's sentiments for Françoise never were reciprocated. Claudette hated your great-grande-tante, and she never pretended to hide it. Just a few months after Claudette's arrival, she became pregnant.

"While time froze for Françoise, it didn't stop for Claudette. She gave birth to twins, a boy and a girl. She named the daughter Joana, and the son she named Michel. She always said it was after her parents, for she believed they had been there beside her in spirit throughout her pregnancy and during the delivery to protect her from your great-grand-tante Françoise's envy, jealousy, and sorcery.

"Just a few months after Claudette gave birth, your great-grand-tante became pregnant. She begged Jonathan to keep the news secret until it became time for her to give birth. Unfortunately, when it came time for her to give birth, Claudette purposely refused to take the news to your great-grand-uncle; he was away selling fish and chicken in order to earn more money for his third child. Françoise gave birth on her own, and at forty-three years of age, she was too weak to endure the delivery, so she died. A couple of weeks later, the baby also died, from yellow fever.

"This left your great-grand-uncle broken into irreparable pieces; he began to drink heavily, and he died in his sleep after drinking too much. The people of Jacob believed that he was poisoned by Claudette, who had planned for years to run away with her two children back to Drolline to her parents' house."

I got up from my seat, overwhelmed by the story. Tante Gisela touched my left cheek, saying, "You look hungry; why don't I get you something to eat."

She returned to the house to get me food while I stayed outside, lost in my thoughts, wondering what a witch Claudette truly was to cause my family so much pain and anguish. If only she had still been alive, I would have given her a good piece of my mind, but she was no longer around for me to tell her exactly what an evil person she truly was.

Tante Gisela brought out a dish filled with green vegetables and white rice. I took the spoon and began to eat a little bit faster than I usually ate at home. My day at Tante Gisela's house was going very well, except for the sad story of my great-grande-tante Françoise and great-grand-uncle Jonathan, which preoccupied my curiosity. I could feel an instant bond between Tante Gisela and I, and I enjoyed her presence profusely. I didn't want to leave her, but the sun started to go down and I had to prepare myself to leave before dark.

I prepared to leave her house; she asked me to wait for a few minutes, and when she returned, she had a blue necklace in her hand and handed it to me. I was touched and moved; that necklace looked familiar but I could not remember where I had seen it. Tante Gisela said with a firm voice, "It belonged to your mother. I happened to snatch it away right after she died."

I felt weak once again; I told Tante Gisela how thankful I was that she gave me Maman's most favorite thing in the world. Maman had the necklace, ever since she was a little girl, and here I was receiving it as my own. Tante Gisela told me to wear it and keep it safe.

Tante Gisela and I then separated with a hug. I left her house at once after we hugged, because certain moments are too unbearable. I went home to be with my brothers and my sister. Life was once again filled with feelings of hope. After I came back from my visit to Tante Giselle's house, I no longer carried a heavy burden as I once did. Life seemed to appease me somehow.

By the end of my second year in Le Bleue, I made two new friends. Their names were Helene and Anne. Anne was my age, and Helene was only two years older than me. Through them, I was able to learn more things than I ever imagined I could learn. They taught me how to plant roses soon after meeting them, and they taught me to stay away from the boys who were both rude and dishonest in their speech. They also would have taught me how to swim, but then the weather became too cold to swim in the river. I did not mind this at all, since I did not want to go back to the deep, dark cold water that nearly took me away for good and forever just months after my arrival in Le Bleue. Helene lived with Madame Pauline, who was her grandmother and only guardian. She spent most of her time helping her sick old grandmother plant spinach, collard greens, kale, papayas, and all colors of roses, with which they decorated their yard all summer long. I was not a big fan of gardening until I met

Helene; she talked about it in such a passionate manner that I soon fell in love with planting fruit, vegetables, and roses.

I have to admit that Helene influenced me; I was drawn to the way she lived her life; she was an inspiration to me every day that I saw her. She spoke about honoring God and her family more than anyone I had ever met, and that impressed me very much. She taught me how to pray every morning. Whenever she slept over my house, she would always keep quiet until she said a prayer.

One day, I accidentally interrupted her while she recited her prayer. That was one of the worst days in my life, because she did not speak to me all day. All my questions to her were met with a cold silence; I guess that was enough punishment for me to never interrupt her ever again during her hour of prayer.

Helene inspired me in so many ways. She taught me tenderness; she always used to say that a man does not want a woman who is too cold or too hot, he only wants a woman who is as tender as the love that a little baby gives its mother. She complained about my ways; she often said I was too blunt, I spoke too soon for my own good, and that was not the way a lady should be. She compared my tone to that of an old soldier who had lost all the passion in life and no longer felt the need to go on. At times Helene's perfect personality became a little bit too much for me, so I found a balance with Anne.

Anne was as religious as Helene, but she was not a fanatic. She saw life as a lesson to be learned; she often said that, we all had to bear sufferings while we were here on earth.

Sometimes when I visited Anne at her parents' house, she would ask me, "Judette, do you not care at all about saving your own soul?"

I would reply, with a defensive tone, that I didn't believe one needed to recite the prayers as much as she did in order to achieve salvation, since God was surely the God of love. I looked outside the window when I spoke those words to her. I don't believe he judges us so harshly, for he already knows that we are weak and have faults, even though we strive to be like good children of his, made in his image.

Helene, who was more of a fanatic than Anne was, would have jumped from her seat to correct me if she had heard that. Anne, however, touched my hand after I told her what I thought of God and his grace. I liked that part of Anne very much; she was always tolerant of my beliefs. She only prayed when there were no other chores to do, such as feeding the three white horses her father, Monsieur Jacque, owned, or going to the supermarket to buy bread and fruit for her mother, Madame Martine.

No matter what, my fondness of both Helene and Anne was unbreakable. I knew we were all very different, and I never tried to change them. Helene believed I should pray more; I spent less time in church and more time playing on the fresh, green grass, complaining of useless matters, and not working like she did. I never doubted her fondness of me, but I knew deep inside Helene wished I was a little bit more like her.

While my friendship with Helene and Anne grew stronger, I spent less time at home, and my sister Julie became worried about this. She promised me one morning that she would cook my favorite meal, believing that would keep me home for the rest of the day and through the evening. Frankly, I never knew that my frequent absence from home upset Julie; after all, I knew that her relationship with Robert was a lot better than the one she had with Arnold, so it never crossed my mind that she was upset by my absence or that she missed me at all. As much as I was flattered by Julie's sentiments, I was also disturbed because I felt happier whenever I spent the day with Helene and Anne, had them sleep over at my place, or spent the night at their home.

Then one night, I heard disturbing news; Anne had left home, and no one, not even Helene, would tell me why she had disappeared. I went several times to Anne's house to ask about her well-being, but her parents refused to speak to me or to answer my questions about her whereabouts.

I became ill; one day, I went to Helene's house, but she had already left to plant peas and beans with her grandmother. I was disappointed but decided to go back to Anne's house one more time and ask what had happened to my dear friend. I left Helene's house and took the road to Anne's house. It had been three weeks since I had seen my friend. I knocked at the door, and it was answered by Madame Martine. It looked like she had been crying. I greeted her with every respect, saying, "Bonjour, Madame Martine."

She responded softly, "Bonjour, Judette, what brings you back here again? I thought I told you Anne no longer lives here with us."

I stood by the door, afraid to take a step forward. "Pardon me, Madame Martine, I understand that you did not expect to see me again, especially after you told me to return no more to this very house, but you must understand, Madame Martine, I do not mean to be rude, rather I care only to learn about Anne's safety, for she is one of my dearest friends. I can't just let her go and forget she once was my friend and move on with my miserable life, for I have only her and Helene as a source of both joy and hope while I remain in the city of Le Bleue."

She shook her head for a few seconds; she gazed at me with a look of hopelessness and pity in her eyes, and ordered me to be quiet, for her youngest daughter, Belle, was asleep. I found my way directly to the living room, thanking her for letting me in.

She insisted, "No need, have a seat and this will be quick." She continued, "Anne is gone, our dearest daughter Anne is gone, it has been more than three weeks, and I wouldn't count on any luck in this world to reunite you with her."

My eyes opened wide with shock, and pain stabbed my stomach when she said that Anne was gone forever and that nothing in this world could reunite us.

Madame Martine continued her dry speech, "More than three weeks ago, Anne's father found her laying in bed with a boy; she was naked without shame, as if she did not know better than to bring sin and disgrace into this family. Jacque and I decided to talk to her, thinking that maybe it was a terrible misunderstanding, but Anne confessed to us that she was well aware of what she was doing, and she felt no guilt or remorse because she was in love with this young boy."

I breathed in quickly, telling myself that this couldn't have been Anne's idea, she must have been tricked into doing whatever she did. This matter was not the end of the world, I could fix it, but only if I could see Anne and reach out to her.

Finally Madame Martine stood up and sighed; she looked me in the eyes, hoping to find some hidden truth, and then she said, "Anne was kicked out by her father three weeks ago, he couldn't forgive her. For God's sake, she is only sixteen years of age, and I understand the pain he's going through, seeing her like that; immediately, with no delay, he kicked her out forever." She continued, with a very confident voice, "And maybe it is for the best that Anne is gone; no parents want a shameful daughter, for it is a curse from God."

I felt sick, and I did not want to keep it all to myself. I shouted, "Anne is not a shameful girl! Neither is she gone forever; I will indeed find her, and she will tell me with her own words, what truly happened."

Tears dropped from my eyes again; I felt the weakness I once felt after Maman died, and after losing Karla. Madame Martine's cold words disturbed my mind. I thought, *How could it be? It couldn't possibly be true!* I knew Anne could never do anything of the sort; she was too self-conscious, she knew better than to lay down naked with a boy before marriage, for she valued her body as much as she valued her friendship with me and Helene.

I stopped to catch my breath, and then I ran out of the house. I wondered if Helene knew what had happened to Anne all along;

why would she fail to inform me? Out of all the people in Le Bleue, I wouldn't consider Helene as someone who would hide something that mattered greatly to me, especially when it concerned Anne, my dearest friend.

I ran toward Helene's house. I said to myself, *What's happening to me again? Why is this happening to me again?* Not too long ago, I lost a very close friend; she left while I was still recovering from the death of Maman. Karla had promised to write often, and it had been five years now, and I had not heard anything from her. Did she betray our friendship and find new friends, or was she forced to run away, just like Anne?

I found myself exhausted by my fears. Everything became gloomy, dark, and confusing again. I began to cry out of my misery, I forced tears to come out of my eyes so that the pain I felt inside my palpating heart could be appeased, but despite my attempt to cry, I was not successful. I screamed, hoping someone would hear me and ask me what the matter was, but no one heard me. I stood up from the grass, my dress all muddy from the rain, and began to walk toward Helene's house, hoping she'd be there. I really needed someone to talk to.

I got to her house as it was getting dark. I found her sitting outside by the door; she looked like she had just had a long day herself.

She exclaimed, "Judette, since when do you come to my house all muddy and wet? Are you all right?"

I said, "No, I'm not all right. I wish to know what happened to Anne, and I will not rest until someone tells me what's going on."

Helene stared down at her shoes, looking very calm but uneasy. She replied with an innocent tone, "I do not know what you speak of if it concerns Anne."

I approached her, and she could tell that I was not at all pleased; I took a step as if to walk away. She grabbed my hand to stop me from leaving, and then she let go, saying, "I will tell you everything I know, but you must promise to never tell a soul."

I thought, *Well, Julie asked me to promise never to tell anyone about her secret, and I have not spoken to anyone about her deep love for Robert, except to God.* I took Helene's hand and reassured her that whatever happened to Anne would remain a secret until the day I died. She smiled, but her smile faded quickly as she began to speak of Anne. She held her hands tight together and said, in a very clear voice, that Anne had been adopted. When she discovered the news, her heart was broken. She took leave to go to the city of Palade to find her birth parents.

Madame Martine, aggravated by this, decided to make up a shameful reason for her disappearance. She warned Anne that she was going to tell the world the lie she told me, which would make it harder for her to ever come back. Anne's words to her were, "Go ahead and do as you please, for God alone will judge you and not I."

Madame Martine called her an ungrateful little brat as she left to search for her birth parents. She and Monsieur Jacque disowned her, taking her out of their will; in case Anne got married, no dowry would be given.

I interrupted Helene, saying, "I understand why Anne did what she did. Do you?"

Helene replied with confidence, "Yes, I do. Anne needs to find herself. No one can live a complete life until they know who they really are, why they are at a particular place. One must know where they came from, especially when it comes to blood, for one must understand why they look the way they do, talk the way they do, act, speak, cry, sing, and dance the way they do. Everyone come from a source because every life belongs to an origin, whether it's animals, or people."

I asked Helene, "And where did you learn all this? I mean, I've known you for awhile now, but you've never made more sense to me than you do now. What do you mean by origin?"

She continued, "The beginning of a place, time, body, something or someone comes from."

"And what does this have to do with Anne?" I asked.

"A lot," she said. "She would need to know her birth parents, whoever they are, and where they truly came from, in order for her to truly be her own self, not what other people want her to be. Who knows, perhaps she may even fill in a void that she felt for many long years."

I said, "Well, Anne did not seem to have any voids at all, she always carried her hope with her, even when she was not in the church; whenever she got the time, she would recite her prayer. She always thought that was good enough to protect her from hell and bring her soul close to God. Unless you know another reason Anne would want to see her birth parents, I don't find the void of any kind to be the capital reason here."

I stopped, since I found my tone rising at Helene; I knew my frustration was beginning to show, and I did not want her to be the victim. She should not have to pay for my very bad, stressful day. I knew I couldn't do further harm to myself, but it hurt me to find that everyone else had known what had happened to my dearest Anne. To make matters even worse, I thought, she had left without any letter of explanation, no words telling me why she had to leave.

Anne's adopted mother, Madame Martine, had ruined my day with her cruel lies. I felt weak and tired, and I couldn't wait to go home, take a warm bath, eat dinner, read some book aloud so my thoughts would clear up, and tuck myself in my warm bed, with the new sheets that Papa had sent me; they smelled like fresh roses.

My desire to get back home grew stronger, and so I hugged Helene and said good night with a tender voice.

The next day, I had no desire to recollect just how crazy my previous day had been. Helene did indeed cross my mind, but I had no intention of revisiting her after the conversation we had about

Anne. Although I hoped and prayed all morning to hear some good news from Anne, nothing at all came to my ears.

I spent my entire day sitting outside the main entrance of my house, hoping that Anne would show up in some mysterious way and tell me what exactly had happened to her. Regrettably, the sun went down with no word from Anne. Julie was more than glad to see me spend the whole day at home with her, and as much as I enjoyed our girlish chat together, I couldn't wait for tomorrow to come. I had come up with the idea to search for Anne on my own; I was not too certain the idea would please Helene, and I needed to see her in the morning to inform her of my plan.

I did not sleep at all that night, or probably I slept but only with one eye closed. I opened my eyes constantly, looking outside my bedroom's window, hoping the sun would rise so I could get up already and tell Helene about my plan to find Anne. Exhaustion must have gotten to me between three and five o'clock, because I finally fell asleep, and the next thing I heard was my sister's voice telling my little brother Leon his breakfast was ready.

I knew I must have overslept; the sun was shining through the window onto my face. Without further delay on my part, I quickly jumped from the bed and asked Leon what time it was. He managed, with food in his mouth, to tell me it was a quarter to ten.

I found myself repeatedly saying, "Oh no, oh no, my plans are all screwed up, oh no, why didn't anybody think of waking me up? Oh no, Helene must have left already to assist her grandmother; what am I going to do? How am I supposed to find Anne if I don't get Helene to help me?"

Julie stopped me and said, "Calm down at once; go take a nice bath; don't give yourself a headache, for you are way too young for any kind of intrigues that raise your blood pressure."

Surprisingly, I followed my sister's advice; I went upstairs, jumped into the bathtub she had filled with warm water, and took

a very warm bath. After taking a bath, I put on the blue dress that
Julie had washed for me; I was glad that I was not going to leave the
house with the same dress I had worn the previous day. I joyfully
thanked my sister for all her kindness and kissed her cheek.

I put on my brown leather slippers, and the next minute I was
outside, inhaling the fresh air and picking daisies while they still
looked and smelled fresh; I hoped to give the daisies to Helene when
I got to her house.

When I got to Helene's house, she was standing outside, looking
lost in her thoughts but still carrying the innocent, fresh face that
she always carried with her, whenever I saw her.

I often thought that Helene looked like an angel; ever since I met
her, she always wore a long dress, she treated her long reddish hair
with extreme care, she never lost the purity in her eyes (even when
she was really upset), and she possessed a rare serenity whenever she
was lost in her thoughts like when I arrived at her house. She smiled
when she saw me; we both hugged each other warmly. I handed her
the daisies I had picked for her, saying, *"Elles sonts a toi.* (They are
yours.)"

Her smile became even wider, her cheeks more red than ever.
She exclaimed, "You are a great friend, and I wish Anne was still
here with us."

I instantly withdrew my hands from hers, looking both sad and
guilty, and said hesitantly, "She could still be here with us, Helene,
just like all the old times we spent together, remember? We only need
to find out the name of the city where she resides now, the family
she stays with, or even a single clue of where she has been ever since
she left Le Bleue, and if we could find out all these things, then we
surely shall find her before things get any worse. And when we do
find her, we can probably convince her to come back with us."

My excitement became as high as my hopes were, but Helene
remained silent for several minutes; it was never a good sign whenever

Helene gave a silent response to any type of suggestion or question. It was rather best whenever she expressed her opinions, feelings, and thoughts than when she didn't.

A few minutes later, just when I found myself giving up on her, I heard her breathe hard, and then she said, "Well, it seems to me if we are going to find Anne, we will need some money, in order for us to buy some food and water for the road." She smiled and continued, "Because it appears it'll be a very long day for us today."

I screamed, "You're going to come? You are agreeing to come? Oh my God, I can't believe this, this is unbelievable!"

She replied, "I know, but Anne is our friend, and we owe this to her. We must find her and reassure her of our sincere friendship."

Helene and I jumped in circles, holding each other's hands, exclaiming our joy out loud, which was then interrupted politely by Helene's grandmother, who wanted to know what the big excitement was all about.

Helene answered her grandmother's question before I got the chance to reply. Helene was brief in her response, she told her grandmother we were going to look for Anne. I waited outside while Helene arranged a bag of fruits and two bottles of fresh water for the road. She also took some money that her grandmother had given her on her previous birthday. We both kissed her grandmother on both cheeks and said good-bye, as she watched us wave back at her as we faded from her sight.

The journey was more demanding than we anticipated it to be; after walking for only two hours, we ate all of the pears and apples Helene had packed. We sat and rested on a big rock for more than forty-five minutes so Helene could recite her prayer; I prayed along with her this time, since I felt the need to be protected by God. Helene was impressed that I was reciting the prayer by her side. After the prayer, we noticed that our bottles of water were almost empty, and we searched for the nearest market to buy some water.

We had brought along a picture of Anne, so we could ask the people on the road if they had seen her, and we hoped our next stop would be our first opportunity to ask about Anne. We walked for another mile, and then another mile followed, still with no luck finding a shop to buy bottles of water, and food to eat. We became hungry, tired, and anxious to find a market.

I thought to myself, If it were up to me, we could have stopped in some strange house to ask for some water to drink and rest for a while, but Helene refused to have us talk to strangers. She worried that Le Bleue was not a city to risk it; rather it was filled with dark magic, evil, witchcraft, rape, killing, blood sacrifices, and kidnapping. No mercy was given to those who showed signs of ignorance, weakness, or helplessness in this city.

I, being from the city of Jacob, had heard certain tales and stories that seemed to be true, rather than just old myths that Maman told me as a little girl. I had to learn to accept that they weren't just old stories that I once listened to as a little girl, indeed they were very much true, and I didn't try to go into further details as Helene and I walked, because I didn't want any fear to take possession of me.

I knew Helene was a child of God; she had proved it to me several times, in her beliefs and the mercy she showed for the poor, the sick, the helpless. Even though I had found her a bit of a fanatic in the past, as we were walking, I soon found reassurance being with her. I knew if God protected Helene, then he would show favor to me also as Helene's dearest friend.

At the same time, I wondered whether Anne had found herself a safe place to sleep, some food to eat and water to drink, and people to protect her from the cruel, cold, and unmerciful city. Since I moved from Jacob, mercy wasn't easily shown by the people of Le Bleue, where kindness was prohibited to strangers, black magic was used to persecute others, and many people sought protection from witchcraft.

Finally we reached a huge market; it had everything we needed, both food to eat and water to drink. The market was considered one of the grandest markets within the city.

Helene took my hand in hers, and then she said quickly, "Let's cross the street so that we can get in line before everyone else does."

We rapidly crossed the street; it was a big street where one could get lost easily if one was from out of town, and every evening, tourists and big trucks filled that street, which was called the street of Saint Cecil, because a humongous church, was built there. The people of Le Bleue spent an enormous amount of time and money to build that particular Church; it took them approximately twenty years to finish its construction.

When we entered the grand market, Helene picked out two bottles of water, four apples, biscuits, and bread, along with some cheese. We took our items to a woman, who was a very short woman, probably around her late thirties; she spoke French with a very deep accent and appeared to know very well what she was doing. She didn't charge us for the cheese, but she reassured us we needed not to worry, she would take care of it. As much as we did not want anyone to accused of stealing, we took her offer of free cheese as a blessing from God, and we left the market to find Anne.

Luckily for us, the sun was not as hot as we had expected it to be when we left Helene's house. It was now about three in the afternoon, and we had not yet reached our destination.

After purchasing everything we needed for the road, we felt more confident in our search for Anne. We knew by now that it wasn't going to be as easy as we had imagined. We knew very well that trying to find Anne would take all the strengths Helene and I possessed within our hearts, all our energy, courage, and hope. While Helene and I walked, dust covered our feet from the muddy road, and trees moved freely even though the wind carried no strength in it; still I found some relief as Helene told me her dreams. She continued her exclamation with great confidence in both her voice and her tone. Although I hadn't heard an angel speak to me in my dreams before, I felt some sort of connection to her dreams, for her description of them were very clear; she even made it so clear that I started to visualize her dreams about the angels as if they were my very own dreams.

I asked Helene why they did not visit me like they visited her. She stared into my eyes for several seconds; her gaze was both deep and sincere. I felt as if she was trying to reach my soul, find a hidden truth, which I probably concealed for years without my own knowledge. She then found herself turning away from me and said, "My dearest Judette, God speaks in many ways, and many forms, but he mostly speaks out to us, through his guardian angels, when we are ready and prepared enough to be reached out to. God is not forceful, he is rather patient, hopeful, kind, and gentle to all of us, even to those who deny him, he shows his compassion and loving grace unconditionally."

After three more hours of walking, we both felt the urge to stop and grab something to eat and to drink. After our small meal, we began to ask the people around us if they had seen Anne.

A little later, we stopped near a big tree, which covered us with a very nice shade, while Helene and I took a profound pleasure in. We ate more of our fruit, bread, and cheese. My knees were aching from exhaustion; my entire body began to feel the long miles that we had walked.

I sensed the same amount of exhaustion coming from Helene, except she never complained; she viewed complaints as sins, sins that were mostly against God rather against oneself. She thought those who complained about things carried misfortune with them; she always thought it was best to not complain at all, for God knew how much we endured and suffered before we even got the words out of our mouth. Nevertheless, I felt the need to tell Helene that I could not walk for another mile; I needed to rest because of my fatigue.

Helene took my suggestion into consideration, and we sat underneath another tree; it wasn't as big as the previous tree, but the shade was very helpful, as we ate more food while Helene and I chatted some more about our dreams. It was about six in the evening, and Helene and I needed to find Anne before the sun went down and the blue skies darkened, for she and I feared greatly what would happen if we were in the street real late, alone, with no place to spend the night or the courage to walk the streets of Le Bleue by ourselves in the dark.

We knew we had to act quickly. Helene grabbed Anne's picture from her small brown purse; before I could catch my breath, she saw a tall man near where we were standing and called out to him. The man seemed willing to help two young girls who obviously looked like they were in search of someone. He approached us with a very wide smile, while Helene and I held each other's arms tightly, uncertain of what the man may do to us. Helene must have had more courage than I did, because she managed to ask the man if he had seen the girl in the picture.

Unsurprisingly, he said that he hadn't. My heart raced, and my teeth chattered while my hands were sweating. I quickly whispered in Helene's ear, "Let's get out of here, I don't think he knows where Anne is, and I don't think he'd help us. He may not be safe at all."

Helene quickly thanked him. I felt her squeeze my hand and instantly understood the sign she made. Without wasting another minute, we left as fast as we possibly could. We walked for another mile, and then we saw a huge sign that said *"Bienvenue a la ville de Lebron* (Welcome to the city of Lebron)." We both panicked at once, for we didn't realize we had been walking that long; it was almost seven in the evening, and we found ourselves in a city neither Helene nor I had ever been in, and our search for Anne was nowhere near success. I could feel Helene's fear as her expression became as panicked as mine.

She stopped me for a minute, sighed, and then said, while her voice cracked with both anxiety and nervousness, "Judette, have we gone mad?" She stared at me directly and asked, "What are we doing all the way here?"

I agreed with her sudden worries and thought that maybe this time we had pushed it too far, we had gone way too far; there was probably no way of going back if we didn't stop ourselves now, while we were still at the intersection between the cities of Le Bleue and Lebron. I thought, *What if we can't find our way back at all, what we'll we do then, what will become of us, what will Julie tell our father?*

Questions surrounded my brain; the more I thought, the more fear rose in my stomach, Helene's hand sweating in mine, while my hand sweated in hers. I caught Helene's voice murmuring, "We can't do this, this is dangerous, we have to get back to the city. What if something happens to us, what'll our families do, how will they manage?"

At that point, I knew our trip to search for Anne was over. Helene, who I always considered to be smart, hopeful, brave, and close to God, was now invaded by doubts and fears. So was I, but my greatest fear was seeing Helene become afraid of the outcome, for it wasn't like her at all. As much as I detested giving up the search for Anne, I had to give up. The demands were great and the risk of our own security was too high indeed. Helene and I were still too afraid, naïve of the world around us.

I told Helene, "Let's find our way back to our homes, where our families wait for us impatiently with love, care, and a full life of stories to share with us."

In response, Helene only said one phrase until we returned to our homes, and that phrase was, "May God who is gracious in his deeds protect Anne now, and forever."

Helene had no way of knowing that Anne would never be seen again, but her words did prove to be true. Helene and I returned to the city of Le Bleue. I didn't know much about Helene's state of mind, since she was not one to complain. As far as I was concerned, I felt like a failure, I imagined more and more as each day passed by that Helene and I should have done more, we could have gone farther to find Anne instead of giving up so easily like cowards.

Despite this disappointment, Helene and I found ways to entertain ourselves; she and I were growing up faster than anyone expected. Helene was now twenty and I was looking forward to my eighteenth birthday, which was only a few months away. I was excited, excited about having gone through so much in the last years but still standing.

I was even more excited to notice that my breasts were increasing in size as the years went by. Helene by now was already talking about marriage, even though I was far from being interested in the subject. I always believed marriage was a prison that one could never get out of, once the sacrament was completed.

Julie's love affair with Robert had gotten better as the years went by. I stopped assuming that she was going to wake up from her world of illusions and finally end it all with him. Papa kept us in his thoughts through his warm, loving letters that he constantly sent to us, but at times even that appeared to be insufficient. I wanted to see him, run to him like in the old days, when he could still lift me up, when I was still small, with a warm smile and an adorable face, filled with innocence.

Following Papa's wishes, in the fall, Julie enrolled me in a new school; it was called the La Femme De Coeur. I didn't much enjoy all the rules of my new school; all the girls were obligated to follow the rules without any protests, although those rules at times were broken by some of the girls, especially those with more experience than me. Whenever the school board learned that a rule had been broken, a large fee was required to be paid in cash, in order for the school to waive the punishment; at times, if the rule was too grave to excuse, the student was terminated instantly.

I could live with some of the rules but not with Madame Jacqueline, one of the principals. She was a cruel woman; I could never adjust to her brutal tone. She called all the students spoiled little brats who didn't try hard enough in life. She believed everything came too easily to them. I always thought to myself that she mustn't have been talking about me at all. From what I recall, I had it hard. I had it harder than I ever wanted.

Madame Jacqueline's discipline was extremely overwhelming; I used to find her speeches cold, demanding, and harder than the geometry exercises that Monsieur Pierre gave us each Monday morning, but I forced myself to adjust to her inhuman rules. I had to make Papa more proud of me once more. Papa's decision to send me to a new school was based on my poor performance and lower grades that I had received in the years since Maman departed.

After I left for school, Helene visited me on weekends; she brought me several handmade scarves and sweaters to match my dark green uniform; they also kept me warm during the cold weather. She wrote to me constantly about how much she missed me ever since I left home. Only a few months after my arrival at La Femme De Coeur, I heard the sad news of the death of Helene's grandmother. One cloudy Friday morning, the sky was still grey and you could barely see the clear blue colors in them. Monsieur Maurice, who was one of the principals, informed me that Julie had called his office on Helene's behalf to inform me that Helene's grandmother had passed away; she had departed to find her peace with God, accompanied by good angels.

I sat down, weakened and defeated. I understood just how hard it must have been for Helene, and I knew how her life was going to change forever. I had lost my mother; therefore, I have come to know how deep the heart bruises itself once the sustainer of love it once occupied ceases to live. I have been blue to my deepest bones with no sun to brighten my face and soul. I have seen the enormous damage that occurred in the past years, friends who had left my life without warning or the desire of ever returning to where I was. I thought nothing came so easily, and in that extent, nothing seemed to remain forever on our sides, even when the intentions to keep a loved one so close were very well intended.

It was as if death had a mind of its own. It doesn't choose who it will take next; it doesn't show compassion, even to the weakest soul, such as that of a baby or a poor old woman like Helene's grandmother. I remained sitting while thoughts of agony and regret invaded my mind. I could not stop my thoughts from taking me to the depths of fear; time went on as usual, I heard noise in the background of my building, but my ears got lost somewhere along with my thoughts, so that I no longer recognized the voice of Clarisse, who was in the same history class as I was.

I found my way back to consciousness very slowly; Clarisse was screaming loudly, "Judette, open the door! Judette, are you in there? Open the door. Do you not remember that we have a history assignment that we are to complete today? It's due tomorrow."

I reached outside the window, forcing myself to stand up from where I had been sitting for approximately two hours without movement. I opened the window of my room and forced my mouth to say Clarisse's name. I managed to call out, "Clarisse, I'm sorry, I couldn't hear you at all, come around inside the building, and I'll have the door opened for you."

I opened the door for Clarisse; she helped herself in and quickly deposited her jacket on the nearest chair she found in the corner of my room. She asked me, "Judette, are you all right? If not, I could come back another time, maybe find another partner or just work the assignment on my own."

I stopped her before she could add another word or phrase in her talkative tongue.

"No," I said, "it's all right, everything is fine. I was just having a midday rest, for I knew you were coming and wanted to rest before you came."

She responded, "Good, well, I'm here; shall we begin?"

Clarisse and I both reached for our history books and read the first thirty pages about the first war the country ever encountered. We also had to answer questions about the outcome of the war. It took Clarisse and me a good three hours to finish our assignments, and then Clarisse gave me a new pen; she promised it'd bring me good luck whenever I used the pen during exams.

I took the pen but wished that Clarisse would leave so I could go back to my thoughts, the only place I could recapture the lost years and console Helene's sorrow. Clarisse soon departed from my room; I then found myself wishing that I could see Helene and give her my condolences like she and Anne used to give me when I first met them. I can still remember their voices, calm with concern, expressing their most profound and sincere regrets when I informed them about the illness that took Maman permanently away from me.

I recalled telling Anne and Helene that my heart felt as if it never existed, my soul was cold, my words were bitter, my thoughts and feelings were dark because of death, a death that one suffered alone with both eyes opened.

The remembrance of their great comfort toward me made me want to go back home and be of assistance to Helene; she was the only friend I knew who had stayed with me through hell and paradise. Even though we both shared different perceptions of thoughts and beliefs, I knew Helene was my one and only dearest friend. Although words of love were rarely spoken, she knew that I loved her dearly, and I knew that she loved me also very dearly.

My thoughts were now firm. I had to write a formal letter to Monsieur Maurice, requesting him to grant me permission to take immediate leave so I may share my strength, comfort, and hope with Helene. My letter was written, my mind already made up, my anticipation to reach home already built up at each minute, and the desire to stand by Helene's side rushed through my warm blood, while I wept softly.

It was now two in the afternoon; I finished my letter to Monsieur Maurice. I wrote, *"Dear Monsieur Maurice, as you already know by now, since you, yourself, brought to me the sad news of the death of Madame Pauline, who happened to be my dearest Helene's grandmother and only guardian. The sad news has left me both possessed with grief and scattered. I believe with all my heart, it would do both Helene and I much good to be close to each other at such a devastating time."*

I signed my letter neatly at the bottom of the page. I rushed out of my room to the school's market to purchase an envelope, thinking the more formal my letter was presented, the better chance I had to get permission to take my leave. When I reached the school's market, I not only purchased a box of envelopes but also a charm bracelet to give to Helene for courage. My trip to the market was not as demanding as I imagined it to be. I spent only twenty-five minutes to do everything that I had left my room to accomplish.

When I returned to my room, I folded my letter in three, inserted it into a new envelope, and left to give the letter to Monsieur Maurice.

When I reached Monsieur Maurice's office, I saw only Mademoiselle Catherine, Monsieur Maurice's secretary; she was also his mistress, at least that's what I heard when I first arrived at La Femme De Coeur. The gossip that circulated was that Monsieur Maurice cheated on his wife with Mademoiselle Catherine, who was only twenty. Whether or not this gossip was true, I often heard students whispering in the school's hallway that Mademoiselle

Catherine was once caught giving Monsieur Maurice a very affectionate kiss on the mouth inside his office.

The story always disgusted me for Monsieur Maurice was too old to be dating a twenty-year-old; that was the least of my concerns, I was more upset about his poor wife, who sat faithfully at home waiting for him to return home from work, and his reputation if the affair ever reached outside the school; how was he to manage such a disastrous outcome?

When I reached Monsieur Maurice's office and saw Mademoiselle Catherine sitting at her desk, glowing and looking beautiful as always, I handed her my letter without asking to see Monsieur Maurice. I thought, *Poor man, he got trapped for sure.*

I could see that Catherine was a very beautiful girl, she was more beautiful than I had imagined, in accordance from what I've heard the girls in my classes say about her beauty. She carried a seductive look with her, she knew just how beautiful she was, I could read the arrogance and vanity that her face expressed as she said, "I will make sure that your letter gets to Monsieur Maurice once he returns from his meeting."

Not wanting to read more expression on her face, I rapidly thanked her and rushed out of her sight, before she became suspicious of my intense gaze toward her. My heart broke even more when I reached my room. I began to wonder if being in love meant only living with someone's lies, or better yet, was love just one big lie, formed in the act of pretence and hypocrisy? I'm sure Monsieur Maurice's wife was a very good-hearted person, even though I knew nothing about her, and here in the school her so-called good husband was proudly cheating on her with a girl who was twenty years younger than he was.

My sister Julie went through the same trauma just weeks after Maman left. Although she had given her heart and soul completely to Arnold, apparently that was not good enough for him; he showed no hesitancy to be with another woman, he deliberately took the opportunity he got and cheated on Julie with no second thoughts whatsoever.

Poor Julie, I thought, as I recalled what that useless Arnold did to her heart. I reminded myself it wasn't time for that; I wasn't going to question the nature of love. It wasn't in my bones to understand how or why people fall in love; if it's been clear for so many centuries that love comes with indescribable pain, which carries no remedy of any kind whatsoever, then who was I to solve this issue of humankind?

I stood in silence, looking outside the window; I could count every single mountain that faced where I was standing in my room. I waited for a response to my letter from Monsieur Maurice; hours went by, and I watched the time on my clock go by without hearing any word from Monsieur Maurice's office. I decided a nap would do me more good at this point than just sitting around and observing my troubled heart collapse into nonrepairable pieces.

After napping for about an hour, I was awakened by a hard knock at my door. I opened my door; surprisingly, it was Mademoiselle Catherine herself. She had changed into a different outfit than the one she wore this afternoon when I first saw her. She now wore a tight sleeveless pink dress, with black high heels. She managed to make herself look much older than she was, her sparkling blue eyes shined as bright as the light of the evening star when she smiled.

She asked with a warm smile if she could come in my room. I nervously responded, "Yes, of course, please come in."

She looked around my room as she made her entrance. I felt real small in comparison to her beauty, and after a few minutes of silence, she said, "I've come here in person in regards to the letter you wrote to Monsieur Maurice concerning your desire to take leave for a couple of days to assist a friend of yours who has lost a very close relative. I felt it was best that I come to your room in person to inform you that he has given you three days to go home and to be with your friend, and he wishes you and your friend Helene courage and healing."

I wanted to cry out with joy and exclaim how happy I was, but I felt it was better to wait until she was gone. Mademoiselle Catherine left my room immediately after she delivered the good news to me. I went to Clarisse's room to ask her if she would escort me to the train station, and she gladly agreed to. I began to pack all the things I needed for my trip inside my green travel-bag. I made sure I had my torchlight, the one Papa sent me last year during Christmas, my hair brush and toothbrush, my brown boots made of real leather, the green sweater Helene made for me just a couple months ago, and finally my money to purchase the ticket.

Clarisse was the only girl with whom I interacted outside my classes. I found her quite reliable in times of need. Her life wasn't like mine; she often told me that life was what you made of it, that it was one's own choice to succeed or to fail, to love or to hate, to be happy or to be sad. She believed the past had nothing to do with the present, nor did the present determine the future. She refused to discuss God and often said that there wasn't enough proof that God existed.

Clarisse never spoke about her parents; whenever I raised that subject, she always stopped me with her sarcasm from going any further. I never pushed her too far with it, for I knew there was a reason behind every secret.

When it was time to go to the train station, Clarisse met me outside my room. She quickly took one bag out of my hand, and got on the bus with me. When we arrived at the train station, there was about thirty minutes before my train was to leave.

Clarisse helped me carry my bags into the station. Soon after our arrival, there was an announcement telling all passengers to start boarding the train. Clarisse helped me purchase my train ticket, and then I got on the train. Before I even realized it, I was in the train, sitting down at last, waving good-bye to Clarisse. I have never forgotten how helpful Clarisse was that day.

Two hours later, the train reached my destination; Julie and Robert were waiting for me in Le Bleue, for Monsieur Maurice had called home to inform my sister that I was on my way. I was really glad to see Julie; I couldn't say the same thing about Robert, but I was profoundly grateful that he picked me up with his father's Mercedes. I thought it was very kind of him. As glad as I was to see Julie, I was a little reluctant to meet with Helene and discuss her sorrow, which was nearly my own.

When we got home, Robert did not hold back on giving Julie a deep, passionate kiss (by now he had gotten used to me); I would say the kiss probably lasted two minutes, which made me miserable. He didn't stop there; he touched her cheeks softly, brushing his nose on hers while she enjoyed every minute of his caresses. I couldn't take any more of their romance; I interrupted as he was about to kiss her again with a very loud, fake cough.

He took her hand and tenderly helped her out of the Mercedes; as Julie slowly got out of the car, he grabbed her by surprise and kissed her again, and this time he kissed her very softly and tenderly. His mouth treated her lips like a rose's petal, as if he was too afraid to press his lips too hard against hers.

I found myself lost for a moment, just looking at them and wondering how it feels to be kissed by a boy. I felt it was useless to thank Robert for the ride, since his attention was totally directed on Julie. Now I understood why Julie spoke the way she did about Robert. It was very clear to see that Robert was very good to her— he saw her as his princess, he sheltered her with love and affection, and he even protected her. I was sure of that just by looking at how tall and strong he was; his muscles rippled underneath his white short-sleeved shirt. I no longer saw Robert as just an unattractive young man who got on my nerves; I spent several minutes observing them both and watching his hands go through Julie's long red hair.

He became suddenly very new to my eyes; I no longer felt the boredom that I used to experience every time I saw him, and he made my sister laugh very hard (she laughed harder with him than she did with anyone else). He made her blush whenever he looked into her eyes. He promised her his everlasting love and protection; he stood outside the Mercedes and held her in his arms, as if to protect her from all of the danger in the world. I thought, *I guess she had me fooled, or I probably just fooled myself. This is how love must feel, and these are the definite signs of love. This is how love truly expresses itself: through endless passion, profuse laughter, warm caresses, and the constant desire to protect the other from all harm.*

I got out of the black Mercedes without disturbing the two lovebirds from their intimate moment. I picked up my bags, but before I could proceed, I heard a voice call my name. I turned back to see who it was; it was Helene. She had lost some weight, but she looked even more beautiful now than ever; she greeted me with a warm hug and two kisses on each cheek.

I grabbed her hand to show her how sorry I was about the death of her grandmother. My brothers came out to meet me the second they heard my voice; Leon, with his adorable, innocent face and hazel eyes, asked me a million questions about where I had been. I was too emotional to reply to his questions; my heart ached to hear him say how much he had missed me. I hugged him instead, kissing him all over his face as he laughed out loud.

Mark came and interrupted my fun with Leon; he hugged both Leon and me to the point where it became impossible to breathe. Mark was tall and well-built, and he was very aware that God had blessed him with a very handsome face. He never encouraged vanity to take over him, but I knew he always enjoyed all the attention about his good looks.

Jacque, Justin, and Mathieu were not home yet; my sister explained that they were on a school trip to Lebron. Laurent and Laurence snored their way into a deep sleep, Leon wanted to wake them up, but I declined this suggestion for I needed to catch up with Helene. It was clear that she was grieving despite her joy at seeing me home once again. Julie, still too preoccupied with Robert outside the house, didn't disturb me at all. I knew she and Robert were very much in love, I found the idea somehow pleasing for I knew just how hard it had been for all of us ever since Maman departed. Julie had found some fulfillment in Robert's arms; it was comforting that she could find herself lost in the realms of love.

My conversation with Helene began, and I knew that it was going to reach a very emotional height. Helene began explaining to me what exactly had happened to Madame Pauline, her grandmother, who had passed away so quickly.

She glanced outside the window, and then she said with a soft voice, "Judette, she couldn't speak for days; there came a time when she refused to have me feed her or even look at her face. She became cold and resentful as her illness got worse. I didn't know what to do or how to react to all the changes she was going through. The doctor had stopped giving her medication; they informed me that it was unclear what kind of illness she was suffering from. I wanted to reach out to you, but I did not want to add worries to your studies, so I gave it all into God's hands, praying desperately that God would show Grandma Pauline mercy and heal her from her misery.

"Luckily I had your sister Julie's assistance, she came and visited Grandma whenever she had time to spare, she brought her vegetable soup on the weekends to boost her appetite. It didn't help at all, but I am eternally grateful toward all that she has done for me and for Grandma.

"Oh, Judette," she sighed as she continued to talk, "if only you had been here on the day that she departed. I thought constantly, surely the pain wouldn't have been as grave as what I felt on the day she permanently closed her eyes."

I had known Helene for several years now; I could feel certain changes that had happened since I departed for school. She was more open than ever about her feelings and emotions; I wondered if this was good or just another breakdown on her part. I wanted to interrupt some of her speech, but I thought it was best that she spoke what she felt in her heart rather than keep it all concealed.

It was getting late; we couldn't get enough of our talk, and Robert by now had left already. I wondered how Julie was going to survive the night without him, since she had grown to love him profoundly. Helene and I quickly found ourselves in my old room, where I listened to Helene recite her prayers; to please her heart even more, I showed more interest in her prayers than I had shown in the past. I wanted her to feel my love, care, and support for her. I could easily relate to whatever she was going through. I didn't want her to become like one of those fallen angels who quickly lost their wings after something terrible has happened. I wanted her to become herself again, happy, secure, and willing to dream again. I couldn't bear the idea of Helene feeling hopeless or helpless, I just couldn't. For years, I viewed her as my light, the light that reminded me of who I was, where I came from, and everything I wanted to be. Her light gave me the truth that I longed for, life to breathe, hope to hold on to, and strength to persevere whenever anything went wrong.

Our evening prayers were said and done with; Helene prayed to her guardian angel. She made every one of her humble requests to her. We warmly hugged each other good night with a kiss on the cheek, and then the lights in our room went out. I was exhausted from my long, stressful day; I needed to rest. I deserved it, I thought.

In the morning, I woke up to find Helene and Julie already making breakfast. I offered to help, but they insisted they were fine and that I needed not to worry. Pancakes, sausages, and eggs were ready, finally breakfast was served, and it felt good to be home again at the presence of my brothers, Julie, and my dearest friend Helene. Laurent and Laurence were very happy to see me home again. They found me in the morning, sitting down in the breakfast table. They took great joy in seeing me; I was very glad to see them both. They had grown a couple of inches taller, they both looked handsome in their matching blue pajamas, I was so proud to find them adjusting better than I did when I was their age to all the changes around them.

I was to leave the next day and wanted to be very helpful while I was home. I decided to help Leon with his laundry; I washed his dirty underwear, shorts, pants, sweaters, and T-shirts that he had used in the past week. I was glad to see Leon; he was always full of life. He had not known Maman well enough to miss her too much, which was good at times because I didn't want him to carry the burden I had to carry. I missed her still as I washed Leon's clothes, the smell of her perfume, her long brown hair, her intense look that she gave me whenever I did something wrong, but above all I missed her cooking. She always used to surprise us in the morning with baked cookies, chocolate cakes, and lemonade, which she made for us herself. She was always happy whenever she made something for us; I assumed that was her way of letting us know just how much she loved us.

Leon jumped around as I recalled Maman in my head. As I reached out for the bleach, he surprised me by jumping on my back. I knew he wanted to play, and I didn't blame him at all. I had been gone for months. Meanwhile, Helene and Julie were washing all the dishes we had used for breakfast. The atmosphere of the house was more cheerful than when I left for school. I didn't know this part of life existed; perhaps I had known about it without feeling it at all. I felt my heart heal as I played with my *petit* Leon.

Later that day, Julie told me she was going to invite Helene to live with us; I was relieved that Helene was going to have a source of support, not only in me but also in my family. She could see how pleased I was to hear Julie say that Helene could join us not only as a friend but also as a sister; I would have embraced Julie if only Leon had not attached himself strongly to my lap.

Helene wanted to speak to me in private; I saw it coming because she looked somewhat pale after Julie mentioned that she could join our home and stay with us. When Helene and I finally got the opportunity to sit down and talk; Helene became quiet and couldn't bring herself to tell me what was on her mind. She was sweating and lacked the ability to tell me what was in her sorrowful heart.

My fears quickly returned again. I thought, *Oh no! What's next? Is she going to bail out on me now and refuse my sister's wonderful proposal and move to another city like others have done? Is she sick, since I can clearly see the sweat coming out of her skin like drops of rain?*

I needed to calm myself down, rest from my deep fear, and calmly ask her to tell me what troubled her heart. I presumed this was to be a celebration not just for me but also for her; we should share not only a friendship but also the same home and family, which could bind us and make us inseparable from whatever the future may challenge us with. She finally spoke.

She said, "Judette, I am forever grateful to you and your family for showing me your warm hospitality ever since my grandmother departed, but I can't help but worry that my presence here will become a great cost in time; I may never be able to return the kindness you have shown me. Although I long to stay until your next visit, I have no other choice but to reject your sister's kind offer. I will join the church, I plan to become one of the sisters of the church in order for me to better serve God and the city of Le Bleue."

I thought she was mad; that thought immediately transpired into an exclamation, as I said aloud, "Are you insane? Or better yet mad? Have we not learned what Anne's departure did to you and to me? Does it always have to end sadly? Must we always say good-bye? Can you not see that you are my only best friend? As I speak to you now, I cannot afford to see you leave permanently, for I am too weak to survive if you leave. Helene, please, don't leave! I love you, you are like a second sister to me, please do reconsider whatever you're thinking. Take the words of good-bye out of your mouth and swear to never ever speak of them, for even the slightest mention of them hurts."

She stood and walked away without saying another word; I was too crushed to go after her. I thought, *What happened? What changed? What's going on? Did I say something to offend her? Did I do something to make her want to go away? Is she thinking clearly? If so, why doesn't she think of what it will do to me if she leaves? Did she forget so soon how awful it felt when Anne left us and never returned?*

Many questions invaded my head; I didn't know how to respond to these questions that crossed my worried mind, or better yet how to deal with the news Helene had just given me. I thought, *Maybe she'll come to her senses once I give her enough space to reflect on my concerns.*

I left Helene alone to reflect on her decision to join the church. I was very disappointed and went to let Julie know that Helene did not want to stay with us. I did not know how Julie would react to the news. I myself was obviously not pleased with Helene's decision to reject my sister's proposal, but I knew I couldn't force Helene to do something that she did not wish to do. As much as I had dreamed for years to live with her as a sister in the same house, I couldn't just make her stay. That was a choice for her to make.

I sat down with Julie and informed her of what Helene had decided, but I did not have the courage to tell Julie that Helene did not feel she deserved to stay with us and to allow us to care for her.

The next day, I returned to school. Clarisse met me at the train station, and I began to realize that she profoundly liked me, and I started to feel the same way about her. About two weeks later, I had not heard anything from Helene, but I did receive a letter from Julie, telling me she and Robert were now engaged.

I was not at all surprised by my sister's engagement; I knew just how much in love they were, and I was very pleased to learn that Julie was finally getting all the happiness that she deserved. I may not have liked Robert in the beginning of their relationship, but I grew in time to accept and respect him, just seeing how secure and very happy he made my sister. It was as if they were meant to be with each other from the time God created the earth and the heavens, despite the great contrast I found in their looks and figures. I thought Julie must have been the moon and Robert the sun; they understood one another in a way I never imagined was possible.

They met at the darkest time of Julie's life, just when she thought love was no longer possible, after feeling anger and despair because Arnold had betrayed her, and feeling that love was only an illusion, not sincere or real. Just a little while after her breakup with Arnold, Robert came along like a saving grace to share his path with her, and since then, he became her light, her fire, and the question remained if the light he gave her, or the path he chose to share with her, would last forever.

I wanted so desperately to experience the results of their love and relationship once they were married. Meanwhile, my adjustment at La Femme De Coeur was not going as well as I wanted. I still hated how the girls at the school whispered and gossiped. They couldn't get enough of Monsieur Maurice and Mademoiselle Catherine's love affair; it became the main subject until she transferred to La Valentine's School. Monsieur Maurice did not stay long after Mademoiselle Catherine was transferred; he also requested to be transferred to another school. I never learned whether Monsieur Maurice and Mademoiselle Catherine were reunited, but Clarisse did inform me that he filed for a divorce a few months after he left. She said his wife rapidly granted his request.

Until then, I knew little of love, marriage, and relationships; I could not understand how Monsieur Maurice could shatter the commitment and the promises he had made to his former wife, with no remorse on his part whatsoever. I could not analyze what he had done or why he had done it. I also could not pass judgment on Monsieur Maurice, for I knew the weakness mankind carried right beneath the flesh.

My inability to understand why Monsieur Maurice had left his wife did not prevent me from feeling great sorrow for her; I heard she had been in love with him ever since they were eleven years old. As a young girl, she was very much determined to make Monsieur Maurice her husband; I questioned myself at times if she had been so blinded by her ambition to fulfill her childhood dreams that she did not verify if he had wanted the same thing too. Life, I thought, was a challenge on its own, and love was a subject I would find out about later.

Clarisse and I managed to keep ourselves out of trouble, and we were lucky enough to stay out of the exterior influences of gossip, and the usage of witchcraft. Witchcraft was a popular practice in Le Bleue, especially in La Femme De Coeur School. Girls in my school often used charms to influence a particular person and gain what their heart so desired. Clarisse and I never believed in those practices, even when some had tried to forcefully involve us in them; we had faithfully refused on many occasions.

Unlike the way I used to be, Clarisse did believe in love, but she resented the usage of magic, charms, or any practice to manipulate people and their hearts and emotions. She always told me that the consequences were too great for one to achieve love by witchcraft. I understood Clarisse's beliefs very well; I knew she was a good girl, maybe not as good as Helene was, but good enough to keep me away from trouble. I was under the same beliefs as she was, except I did not believe in love; I always thought something must have been terribly wrong with anyone who fell in love; that's what I thought before I met Ethan, the love of my life (at least that's what I believed he was).

Meanwhile, Helene kept me guessing for six straight months; her strange silence worried me, but I was reassured by Julie's words. She wrote to me many times that Helene had not gone to join the church, instead she remained with my family. I was unable to comprehend what had changed her mind, but I was glad to know that she did not leave home at all.

In mid-December, Helene finally wrote me a long, warm letter; she described her life in our home as a blessing and said that her feelings for my brother Mathieu had grown into love; her feelings were strong enough to know that it was truly love itself speaking to her heart in many forms. I was delighted to learn this news, but I was also confused by the idea of them together. I was hurt that she had remained silent for so long, and I was hurt because the precious time that she had shared with me in the past years was now taken away by her love for my brother Mathieu.

Her letter was two pages long, and both pages were filled with words of love; as confused as I was, I was not too surprised to read her letter, which resembled a poem, and not just any poem. I replied to her letter right away, reassuring her of my support and great joy to learn that her heart now had a reason to live. As far as I was concerned, I was still looking for a reason to give in to love without the agony of regrets, and until I found that reason, I did not have a reason such as Helene's to care for someone else.

I wrote my letter and posted it the next day. The month of January came and went very quickly. Clarisse and I began to hang out with two new girls in our school; they were both self-conceited and had so many things to teach us. I knew little about boys and makeup, and I found a growing desire to look more and more beautiful. I became accustomed to all the things the new girls brought along with them, which was not all necessary or good for one's soul. I was now using red lipstick, powder, and dark eyeliner. I began to apply makeup every morning. It all came too fast and sudden for my own good. I did not prepare myself for what was to happen to me, but the new girls had intruded themselves in my world.

The new girls' names were Alice and Elizabeth; they were not from Le Bleue or Lebron. They both came from Lalliance; I knew nothing of this city except of its great wealth, gold and diamonds. The city was filled with very tall buildings, so tall that people thought they could reach God and the skies through those buildings. The streets were rarely empty, day or night. There were many stories about the city of Lalliance; it was an unholy, dark, and lustful city, but the people there were prohibited from saying what exactly took place there. Women and children were often brutally raped, and both men and women were killed as part of sacrifices and rituals.

Many unpleasant stories circulated in the hallways about the two new girls and also about anyone who came from the city of Lalliance. In my very own naïveté, I ignored all of the gossip, rumors, and stories about Alice and Elizabeth. I would not allow my friendship with them to end over silly myths and inaccurate stories, so I thought.

A new boy had arrived at La Femme De Coeur; his name was Ethan Charles, and later on, Elizabeth introduced me to him during our piano lessons. I lost every inch of my soul and all control that I ever had, for I had never seen a boy as handsome and charming as he was. Growing up and watching Julie's heart get broken into little pieces made me view boys as the most dangerous accessory a girl could have. But as he stood tall before me, his eyes were light brown, and they were as clear, pure, and beautiful as a fairy prince's; his skin was indescribably tanned, for he had lived in a warm city all of his life. He was not too skinny, I thought his weight suited him perfectly. His teeth were extremely white; I found myself inevitably staring at them with the desire to kiss him (or to be kissed by him).

I wondered secretly, hiding my admiration underneath my insecure gestures, if other girls before me had complimented him on his very handsome face and admirable body. He was filled with great confidence, while his face remained both still and intense, and he stood in one spot without making any movements. My heart raced every time I shyly glanced at him. I couldn't resist the idea of being with him; I tried everything from avoiding him in the hallways to changing my piano classes from Thursday mornings to Friday mornings, so that I did not sit too close to him.

As much as I tried to keep him from noticing whatever it was that I was deeply feeling for him, Alice and Elizabeth were also determined to see Ethan and me together. Elizabeth had known him before he came to the school; their families were very close. She arranged for us to meet after school. I did not want to appear desperate, but my heart apparently could not stop thinking about him. I don't know exactly what Elizabeth told Ethan about my feelings, but the next day, she brought me a letter from him. She and Alice giggled as they entered my room. They gave me the letter with huge smiles on their faces. I opened the letter, hiding my excitement; I blushed at each word as I read the letter.

He wrote, *"To Judette, whom the gods had made me love before I was even born, my dearest beauty, I too do feel the same as you do, and my heart aches at every absence of your sight."* He signed the short letter, *"Yours, Ethan."*

With no further hesitance on my part, I joyfully took my afternoon bath; Alice helped me wash my hair, and I borrowed her beautiful white dress, which fit me so perfectly as if it was my very own dress in the first place. I went to the school garden to meet Ethan, who I assumed was waiting impatiently for me.

When I got to the garden, he was already there, standing and looking distant in his thoughts, impenetrable but still very charming in his khaki pants and pure white shirt. I approached him, making sure my warm feelings were not obvious. I greeted him with my hand; his touch felt very cool. To avoid an uncomfortable silence, I nervously asked him about his parents: who they were, what they did, and where they came from.

He responded elegantly, "My father, his name was David, he was a soldier, and he was a good soldier." He cleared his throat and continued, "My father, David Charles, was a courageous man who fought in many wars; after he returned from these wars, he began to manifest bitterness and violent acts toward women. He lost everyone and everything he had ever cared for, his dearest love, my mother, died from a broken heart during his long absence; her name was Brigitte. Four of his sons died while my father was away fighting in the war; only I, your dearest, remained; I was his last-born son."

I blushed when I heard him say "your dearest."

He continued, "After he returned from the war, my father was accused of raping several women and killing several children."

Ethan's father arrived in Le Bleue to erase the past and all the crimes he had committed, in order for him to redeem his soul through a sincere repentance within the Church. I was overwhelmed by the details Ethan shared with me about his parents, especially that of his father. I couldn't relate at all to what he had been through. Although I had lost a mother, fortunately I knew in my heart that my father was not a rapist or murderer, neither was he a brave soldier. He was just a man who lost his other half; without the presence of Maman at his side, he wandered endlessly in the streets of a foreign city.

I anticipated telling Ethan about my parents but waited until he asked me about them. I answered with hesitance, "Well, Maman, my mother, passed away of a complicated illness when I was nine years of age; her doctors in the end gave up on all their tests because her body was not responsive to the medication they gave her. As for Papa" (my voice gained a little bit of clarity when the subject of my father was raised, I wanted Ethan to see how much I loved Papa and how strong and brave of a man I thought he was, even though he was not a soldier like his father), "he traveled to work as an ambassador. It had been his dream to travel before I was even born."

Ethan's face was very much focused on what I was saying, and I liked his entire focus upon every single word that came out of my mouth. I really wanted to let Ethan know more about who my parents were and how hard they had worked to provide us with love, protection, and happiness. For as long as Maman was still alive, I watched her and Papa love each other, despite the little money they had for themselves and for us, their children, and they never once gave up their dream that one day, things were going to get better and we were all going to enjoy life to the fullest.

Ethan smoothly picked a white rose from the garden and gave it to me, saying, "This is for you, my lady; wherever I go, in my mind you remain forever as lovely and as pure as this white rose is."

I blushed at his romantic remark but quickly managed to recover and to appear not too easily impressed. Ethan and I were done with our talk, we knew we had to get back to our rooms before the sun went down, for our new principal, Madame Rosette, was even more strict than Monsieur Maurice had been. Madame Rosette was a perfectionist, she did everything very seriously, she left no room for students who gave excuses each time a rule was not followed, a class was not attended, or an assignment was not completed. She was about forty-five; she may have had a boyfriend but her mean looks made it impossible for us to believe it. She often said that she hated kids and was glad that she never had any. After the students were in their rooms at night and on the weekends, she remained to keep track of everything. Her long blonde hair made it so much easier for students to recognize her walk every time she marched in the hallway. Teachers often complained of how unpleasantly she spoke during conference meetings. It was hard enough to adjust to all the rules La Femme De Coeur required of its students, now I had to deal with Madame Rosette, who took pleasure in embarrassing or insulting students when she spoke to them.

When we left the school garden, Ethan acted like a gentleman and accompanied me to my room; when we reached my room, Alice and Elizabeth were already there, waiting for me. Ethan was very well mannered; before he left, he took my right hand, kissed it warmly, and marched slowly away while I went into my room. Alice and Elizabeth's faces were filled with questions; they clearly were dying to find out what had happened in the garden. Before I could speak, Elizabeth asked, "So what happened? Did he kiss you yet? Or don't you have a clue what I'm talking about?"

I ignored her mocking tone.

Alice's voice followed after Elizabeth's. "Well, Judette, tell us, did your lips touch his? Did he kiss you, or was it all just a waste of time for us to sit here and wait for you until you returned from your first walk with a charming boy?"

I wished then that I had known what kind of girls both Alice and Elizabeth truly were, and the kind of trouble they had in store for me in their vicious hearts; if I had, then I would have been able to read behind their wicked minds.

I nervously responded, "Yes, he kissed me, right on my lips, our lips touched each other, I enjoyed his warm and soft caress." I was so eager to fit into Alice and Elizabeth's world that I lied to them; this lie troubled my conscience, for I feared the kind of trouble it would cause if it reached Ethan's ears.

Luckily, my lies did not reach Ethan; the school had come to the end of the year, and everyone returned home, except me, who waited to have my sister send me the money to purchase my train ticket. Ethan went back to his father's home. I remembered the day his father came to pick Ethan up; he looked as handsome as he had looked the first day I saw him. He wore a white shirt with navy pants; he did not look toward where I was standing, but I understood it was only because his father was talking to him and watching his every move carefully. He probably feared what would take place if his father noticed his admiration of me (at least that's what I told myself in order to console my heart over the fact that he had indeed ignored me).

At last, Madame Rosette received my money for the train ticket from Julie. Madame Rosette's secretary, Madame Moine, delivered my train ticket to my room and I left the same day. When I arrived home, I was very happy to see my family once more. I had missed them all profoundly, and they could all detect it. I was to assist Julie, who was getting married; I was determined to help her achieve her dream wedding.

I was glad to see Helene when I returned from school. She was still living at home with us; I did not find her engaged to my brother Mathieu, as I had feared, but I did find them both still in love, just like she had described in her letters. Helene was the same as when I had left her; she did not change a bit when I saw her after eleven months.

Meanwhile, I kept my mouth sealed about my love interest at the school; I did not want to talk about Ethan to Helene or to my sister, for I wasn't too sure of what the future held. Although I wasn't one who believed in witchcraft, magic charms, or readings to reveal the future, my feelings for Ethan became so strong that I wished I could consult a clairvoyant to know if Ethan was truly my one true love or just a vague fantasy without truth, hope, and stability.

A few days after I got home, Helene and I concentrated on Julie's dream wedding; we began to consult pastor after pastor, looking for a church that met my sister's taste and satisfaction. After a long search, we chose the Church of Saint Antoine.

Julie was very satisfied with the church that Helene and I picked for her; she now decided to have her dress made by Madame de Boie. She refused to wear Maman's wedding dress, saying that her emotions were too weak to imagine the day Maman married Papa. I understood Julie's pain more than I understood my own. Her pain was usually expressed with tears, while mine never shed any tears; I could not cry, I had tried too many times and had failed.

My sister's wedding brought both good and sad memories, but no matter how hard the days got, Helene and I continued to set all the arrangements necessary in order for Julie to have her dream wedding. Papa was still away and had been informed of the wedding; he was so taken by his work that he couldn't attend the wedding or enjoy the joy our family was about to share. He sent Julie money to buy her wedding dress and pay for the cake, food, drinks, and entertainment our guest were to enjoy.

Robert, on the other hand, spent time with his family decorating the church with both white and red roses (that nearly resembled the white rose Ethan had given me at the school garden). My time with Helene was filled with amusements; we spoiled ourselves with sweets, cakes, and drinks while we tried to decide what to serve to the wedding guests.

Then came the list of the people to invite; we had a visualization of a beautiful wedding with about twenty five guests, and Papa had asked Julie to invite the family Monte, the family Laurence, and the family Bordeaux. I felt that Papa had not thought about this request very clearly. The Montes were one of the wealthiest families in the small town of Luke; Monsieur Pierre Monte worked for the newspaper and also worked secretly for the government, who found his way to power by corruption, bloodshed, lies, and dirty deeds. Monsieur Monte had five children, which he helped to manage the city with treachery and lies. Monsieur Monte shamelessly corrupted teachers so that his five children may succeed from school and receive great jobs, without merit.

He had four sons and a daughter. The boys' names were Mathias, Daniel, Roland, and Albert and his daughter's name was Farah.

Farah was now over thirty; many men had asked for her hand in marriage, but none of them kept their promises. I did not blame those men, for she had an attitude that turned one off immediately. Whenever I saw her, she acted as if she was better than everyone else who surrounded her. I believed that God in his abundant justice had not blessed her with beauty to match her great pride and selfishness, because he knew what a disaster she would become.

Similarly, Mathias, Daniel, Roland, and Albert were unbearably ugly; they had tried in vain for many years to buy beauty with their father's corrupted money, the money he stole and stored during many years in the government. I guess his service to the government was very well paid, while his wife, Madame Fleur Monte, spent years of her life pretentiously teaching at Le Ouvrier, as a way to keep their secret lives undercover. They certainly did not want anyone to know that the money they had came from corruption and blood, which they earned by serving the government in secrecy.

Madame Fleur Monte was not the least bit beautiful herself; her face was like a pig's. Her daughter Farah had taken after her mother's bizarre looks; her face always looked plain whenever I saw her. While Monsieur Pierre Monte had none of the charm a man with riches usually possesses, he did have one of the fattest stomachs in town. At times I wondered if he had spent most of his wealth on food or simply just eating frogs all day long. His voice wasn't pleasant to hear; he was not at all attractive in his looks or his manners; and his sons had apparently taken after his manipulation, ugliness, and dishonesty.

Despite his great wealth, and the many houses he possessed, I never paid much attention to his four sons. I was always too taken by how big his stomach was to give importance to his other unmerited accomplishments. Many times, I thought the family Monte were not the kind of family one could take any pride in. They donated nothing to the church, or their friends, but they took every bit of pleasure displaying their wealth to those who were poorer than they were. They claimed they had worked harder than anyone else in the city of Luke.

The family Laurence, on the other hand, wasn't as bad as the family Monte was, but they too at times made one wonder why God created them in the first place. Monsieur Laurence was married, at the age of forty-three, to a twenty-six-year-old prostitute who only loved him for his money. In less than ten years, his wife, Karel, gave birth to four children. Everyone mocked him because she had gotten pregnant quickly in order for her to receive all his money in case something happened to him.

Everyone in the city of Luke knew just how wicked and malicious Madame Laurence was. She had adopted her sister's daughter, and rumors circulated that she starved her niece nearly to death without any food or water to drink; she refused to give her food or buy her clothes or shoes to wear to school.

I had heard that Monsieur Laurence was too much of an idiot and a pushover to notice the terrible way his wife treated her very own niece. Madame Laurence never left a trace of any malicious deed; not only that, she also knew how to mistreat others. In time, she learned a valuable way to deceive her husband with his own money. She would make frequent visits to her best friend Mademoiselle Nadine, where she stored every single coin she stole from her husband. Monsieur Laurence did not suspect anything to be missing from all of his bank accounts.

At last there was the family Bordeaux; they spent millions of dollars without proof of how they gained their money. Monsieur Martin Bordeaux hadn't worked in years, but he purchased three beautiful houses in the city of Le Bleue, and he bought himself four brand new Mercedes. His wife worked at a small shop that sold handmade bracelets. The shop with time gained some sophistication because it started to sell pretty well; still it was way too far from

being authentic enough for one to believe that this was the only way
the family Bordeaux made their living.

The town in which they lived was not too taken by the idea that
Monsieur Bordeaux could buy big, beautiful homes and new cars,
just by having his wife work at a handmade bracelet shop. Everyone
knew that the family Monte, the family Laurence, and the family
Bordeaux had secrets, not just any kind of secret that anyone could
get away with; these secrets were dark, dark to a point where it
became worthless for anyone to try to understand.

Julie's worries concerned me a lot, and I understood her resolution
to not invite the three corrupt families to her wedding. I would have
felt the same way if it had been my very own wedding. Julie did
not compromise very easily, she had a mind of her own, she took
no reservation of any sort when it came to giving out her personal
opinions about what she thought, but we all knew that not honoring
Papa's wishes would have unsuccessful results.

Julie was furious when she read Papa's letter asking her to invite
these three families to her wedding. Money was not to be an issue;
Papa had reassured us many times that he would take care of all the
expenses, and he had indeed saved a decent amount of money and
valuable jewels for her dowry. As much as I found Julie's attitude
and reaction to be correct, I needed to calm her down, which she
did after I gave her some words of appeasement.

I slowly took the letter out of Julie's fingers, placed the letter
beside us, and then spoke very softly, so that nothing I was to say
would aggravate her anger toward Papa even more.

I touched her hair and said, "Julie, you have to look at the
brighter side, you are getting married, you are about to become a
respectable *grande-dame*. You will soon be cherished and worshiped
by Robert, just as I know you have wished for in the past years, and
soon you will be referred to as Madame Charles. You will no longer
be Mademoiselle Julie Pompes. If during the wedding you should

feel some uncertainty or unpleasant feelings regarding the three corrupted families, take a good look at Robert's eyes, as if you were reading his heart and soul, and then all shall be well."

My sister may not have thought of me as very helpful before, but she admitted later that my advice was quite helpful indeed. At their wedding at Saint Antoine, Julie and Robert honored their love before God's eyes; they exchanged their promises to love each other and support one another until God's time came for them to part. The wedding was astonishingly beautiful; the altar was filled with beautiful red, pink, yellow, and white roses; candles were placed at the beginning of each row of seats; and the carpet had fake snow on it, for Julie had always dreamed of seeing the snow.

Julie's long red hair was tied into a beautiful round braid; Julie's beautiful white dress was the talk of the town. When she floated down the aisle in her long dress, she appeared as innocent as an angel. I thought Madame de Bois had made the perfect dress just for her. Papa had sent her an enormous amount of money, in order for her to design Julie a dress that was beyond her imagination.

The family Monte, the family Laurence, and the family Bordeaux did come, for Julie had respected Papa's wishes and sent each family an invitation. They sat in the best seats in the church, as Papa would have liked them to; at the dinner reception, they were very well served, for Julie always took great pride in everything that she did; she was an extreme perfectionist.

All of the guests who were invited made it to the wedding except for Robert's father, who was in the hospital with yellow fever. Robert's mother came to the wedding; she stayed until the ceremony was over. Robert's mother gave Julie and Robert her blessing, and then she took leave back to the hospital to be by her husband's side.

I felt bad about Monsieur Charle's illness, but Julie looked as happy as ever. She looked like she was in heaven, and I had promised her I would enjoy her wedding to the fullest. I ate like I never ate before. Food was in every corner I went and every place I sat. The cooks at the wedding killed several cows, chickens, and goats in order to prepare for the wedding, all kinds of sea food was cooked just for the wedding, tilapia was grilled, catfish broiled, and other nameless fishes that I didn't recognize.

Julie definitely had her dream wedding despite the attendance of the three most annoying families in the world. As I went to bed that evening, my brain recaptured how beautiful the wedding had been; if only Papa had been there with us, walking Julie down the aisle before all people sitting at the church. I thought it had been a great celebration, and I wondered if Maman had been invisibly present at the church, watching over all of us and seeing just how handsome and grown my brothers had become.

I woke up the next day feeling a bit sick and dizzy from all the food and drink that my body had consumed. Helene was still in bed, snoring in a deep sleep. I did not blame her, for she had worked diligently to give Julie her dream wedding. She had created and cooked some of the food, including the best dishes ever of goat meat, while I helped to decorate the church with flowers. Julie only wanted two sets of colors for the wedding flowers, but I had thought that more colors would give the church a cheerful look that would greet each guest at their entrance.

I went to Julie's room, only to find that she no longer slept by herself; it was now her and Robert. Luckily they were not disturbed by my rapid steps. I slowly closed their bedroom door and stepped outside, where I managed to stand for a few minutes until I realized that I needed more sleep. So far my vacation was going along well. I felt a certain joy and accomplishment by helping Julie with the wedding while I tried to keep my thoughts away from Ethan.

Sunday came; I knew Helene wanted to spend time with me, since she and I had not had time to talk privately at all since I came back from school. I owed it to her, I thought. Helene still attended church every early Sunday morning, and I was somehow glad about that. I needed some prayers to intervene on my part. I dressed myself up in her long blue dress; I had borrowed Julie's brown leather shoes, which Helene said matched well with the dress. I added the pearl earrings Julie gave me as a gift on her wedding day. Helene helped place a pearl necklace around my thin neck. I was very pleased that Sunday morning to look as radiant and as beautiful as I had wanted to look ever since I was a little girl.

Helene wore a bright yellow dress, which went down past her knees. I was both surprised and relieved that she no longer felt the constant need to wear long dresses every day of the week; it was really nice to see that she had loosened up a little. Helene wore a set of gold earrings and necklace; they brought out her pretty blue eyes; her shoes were also brown but not made of leather; they made her bright yellow dress appear even more beautiful to the eyes.

Helene and I finished dressing ourselves; my brothers were still in bed, and we had no intentions of waking them up. We figured they needed the rest; after all, the wedding was exhausting. The newlywed couple were now in the kitchen preparing breakfast. I would have stayed to eat breakfast with them, but Helene and I had to leave in less than ten minutes, and we had a long walk.

We walked out of the house proudly carrying our scarves and books on each hand; it felt like the old days when Helene and I took long walks side by side. We walked for a good fifteen minutes until we reached our church; there we attended mass. I did not take my communion, knowing just how much I had kept from both Julie and Helene ever since I returned home from La Femme De Coeur. Helene, who I am sure had nothing to confess, gladly went to the altar and received her communion, although I did not see her drink the wine; she passed on that one, which raised my attention, for it was not like her at all.

After mass was completed, I suggested that we go and lie down on the green grass just like we used to do when we were much younger and when Anne was still a part of us. She agreed to do so only after much pleading, then she looked surprised and began to laugh really hard. She laughed louder than I had heard her laugh since her grandmother passed away.

"What about our dresses, aren't they going to get muddy?" she asked while her laughter did not at all cease. I guess her laughter was contagious, because I began laughing myself, and I couldn't stop. Helene and I started to run carelessly from one place to the next, laughing very loudly, as if we needed that laughter to redeem our broken hearts and our shattered dreams. At that moment, it felt to me as if we were once more little children; my childhood vision repeated in my head as I ran. We didn't need to think of anything else except the joy and freedom of that moment.

We finally reached the spot where Anne, Helene, and I had played many times in the past. Helene's hands reached for mine; I looked puzzled by what would happen next. I wondered if my idea of playing on the fresh green grass was profitable or just another bad idea coming from me again.

Surprisingly, Helene exclaimed, "We can roll from here to there until our dresses' color can no longer be recognized."

I was glad to hear her say this; I fell on my knees on the green fresh grass. Despite the cold weather, I began to roll on the grass, and then Helene followed after me. She began to roll on the grass also, only she rolled faster than I did. The grass was still fresh and green even though the weather had been really cold in the past months. Wet grass touched our faces, leaving dirt that smelled desirably tasteful; it felt as if there was nothing else left in the world for us to worry about. We did not want to think of the past, about Anne, or about Helene's loss of her grandmother. After rolling for about twenty minutes, our heads felt dizzy and we helped each other get up; we both looked as dirty and strange as we hadn't looked in so many years. Helene and I looked lost once we were done rolling ourselves all over the green grass.

We stood steady and quiet until I recalled how life was when I had been a little girl, without the losses that I had gone through; my thoughts kept me from noticing that Helene's eyes, filled with concern, were now staring at me.

She then asked me, "Are you all right?"

I looked away, feeling my eyes already wet from soft tears that were only seconds away from dropping. I said, "Yes, I'm all right, I'm just thinking about certain things that aren't all right."

Helene's voice cracked as she said, "I know, Judette, I know, and maybe this is the way things must be until God decides to change them."

I thought Helene had been blessed with a much greater faith and understanding then I had been, she knew how to make a negative experience into a positive outcome, she always believed that there was a reason for everything that took place, while I saw more of the unfairness and injustice to all the loss and pain that I had experienced with the departure of Maman and two of my dearest friends.

I felt uneasy. Julie was now married; even though she was still living at home, I imagined things would never be the same way as before. Helene had fallen in love before me; knowing how faithfully she carried God in her heart, she was surely not going to wait for me to find a husband so we could be married at the same time. The reality of these changes filled my heart with many worries. Helene continued to give me words of wisdom until I felt relieved. I thought if Helene, who had nowhere else to go and no one else in this world except for my family, could reason positively, then I could do the same. In some areas, I believed Helene had it just as bad as I did, except that she was much stronger and God had blessed her with more strength than I possessed.

Out of the blue, Helene asked, "So tell me, Judette, have you found a love interest at the school?"

Helene's question choked my breath; I could see myself struggling to respond to her question, uncertain to reveal my feelings about Ethan to her. I replied, "No, I have not, but when I do, you shall be the first to find out."

I said the words without confidence; Helene knew that I had not looked in her eyes ever since she raised the question of whether I had yet find a love interest. Her sharp intuition always alerted her whenever I had a secret or hid the truth, so I was soon caught under her trap.

She pinched my cheek and made me look right into her eyes, and when I did, I felt exposed; she smiled as if she could read what was in my heart. She spoke again. "I sense you're not telling me everything."

"Is that so?" I asked, looking paranoid, and Helene replied bluntly, "Yes. There is more inside your heart than you reveal, and I want to know it all; whatever it is, I am your dearest friend; you may need my help."

She continued her persuasion; she took my hand in hers, and then I felt very guilty. I had hoped to keep the truth about my admiration for Ethan a secret, but Helene could see through me.

I said, "If I had not spoken to you about this before now, it is simply because I have no confidence that Ethan and I will be together, and even if we were, his father leaves me no room for hope."

Helene quickly stood from where she sat very close to me and exclaimed, "I knew it! I knew you were hiding something from me."

I asked, "How can you tell?"

She said, "Well, first of all, you were much softer when you arrived this time from school, compared to the last time I saw you. Now you looked like you've been taking better care of your hair and skin, and when you returned to school, you stopped writing to me frequently, Judette, remember?"

I admitted to her remark with a guilty tone. Helene, so filled with questions, continued her interrogation, wanting to know more about Ethan.

She asked, "So who is this young man whom your heart has lost all of its senses to?"

I coughed, feeling trapped by Helene's direct question. I said with reserve, "Well, he's a new boy who just arrived at La Femme De Coeur. He is precisely my age. His father, as he told me himself, was a soldier and fought plenty of wars; those wars left him nearly mad. He is very strict; I know this because Ethan told me himself."

"So how did you meet this new boy?"

"Well, I didn't exactly meet him on my own terms; it was Alice and Elizabeth who noticed my admiration for Ethan, and so they arranged for us to meet. At the time I did not know exactly what they told Ethan regarding my feelings, but I received a letter from him that expressed his warmest sentiments toward me, and the next day he invited me to take a walk with him in the school garden."

By now I could see Helene's impatience rising and clearly beginning to manifest itself on her face. I understood she wanted to know more; for years I had been Helene's closest friend, and until this, I had never told her anything like the story I was telling her. I made sure that I told her everything.

Helene threw me another one of her questions before I could finish what I was telling her. "So what happened once you and Ethan took a walk in the garden? Did he kiss you?"

Oh no, I thought. *What is so important about being kissed? Why does everyone keep asking me if he has kissed me yet?* Only this time, I did not lie when I replied to the question.

"No, Helene, he did not kiss me, neither did I try on my part to kiss him."

"Well, did the two of you kiss at all before you left for vacation?"

Again, I was frustrated by another question about kissing. I raised my voice due to my frustration.

"No, Helene, we did not at all kiss, and I find your question harder than helpful. Ethan and I have not kissed; that does not mean that we will not kiss in the future, and when the time does come for us to share a kiss, I will make sure that the kiss is right and motivated only by love, not some game or vague fantasy."

Helene lowered her voice; I knew what that meant: she was either sad or discouraged by the way I had reacted so angrily to her question.

She said softly, "I was curious, that's all; I'm sorry, I did not mean to aggravate your temper or frustrate you."

"That's all right," I quickly interrupted her so she did not take all the blame on herself.

However, it did help me a lot that she apologized, because it stopped her from asking me further questions. Our day out was over, and Helene and I found our way back home around four in the afternoon. When we got home, Robert and Julie had already cooked dinner; the table was set in order for us to eat together.

After two months, it was time to return to school. My brothers (with Julie's help) made me a good-bye cake. I thought it was sweet that they made me a cake. Leon was not too happy to see me leave; he hung onto the hem of my new dress, which Julie had surprised me with. I was barely able to step outside the door.

Luckily Robert came to my rescue and distracted Leon with a game; for the first time I could see the importance of having Robert around the house. Although he couldn't make everything all right, seeing him help around the house made life easier for everyone. Robert helped me pack my suitcase, my brothers lifted it into Robert's new Mercedes, which his mother had bought him as a wedding gift.

We got in the car, and Robert, Julie, and Helene accompanied me to the train station. Robert purchased my ticket, and I got on board. The entire scene felt too familiar; although Julie and Helene shed tears of sadness while the train began to move, I managed to act brave until we separated.

I arrived at La Femme De Coeur at seven in the afternoon. Alice and Elizabeth, accompanied by my good friend Clarisse, met me and helped me carry my luggage back to my room. They had arrived back at school before I did. I was very emotional when I got to the school, for I hadn't forgotten the heartbreak I experienced at home and at the train station. I was still overwhelmed by all of it, so I decided not to ask anything about Ethan. Alice wanted us to go dancing that night, but I was tired, so she and Elizabeth went; Clarisse had an exam coming up so she stayed in her room studying.

Nothing at the school had changed except for the new paint in the school eatery, which was now blue instead of yellow; my reluctance to talk to Madame Rosette had not changed despite the two and half months I spent at home not thinking about her at all.

Monday morning came; the routine had not been changed, neither did any of the rules. When Madame Rosette arrived in my Latin class, everyone stood in fear (rather than respect) to greet her. I stood just like everyone else in the classroom, while making sure that Madame Rosette did not have an occasion to mock me, since that was something she really loved to do. I often wished that enough students would complain to their parents, who could write letters to her protesting how critical she was.

Madame Rosette did not have good taste when it came to her clothes or appearance; she was very plain, muscular, and careless in her long black dress and overused black leather shoes. She wore no jewelry at all; she gave one the impression of someone who did not like being a woman. She did not seem to enjoy the elegance of being a woman. Madame Rosette walked throughout the classroom, hoping to find defects in the students or the classroom so she could say mean things to us. My heart beat heavily when she reached my range of seats; she stood close to me, making sure that my attention was totally captured by her dominant presence. I knew she enjoyed hearing me breathe hard, for she took pleasure in making others suffer fearfully.

Once my eyes made direct contact with hers, she asked firmly, "Judette, did you enjoy your vacation at home?"

I said hesitantly, "Yes, Madame Rosette."

She continued her walk around the classroom; when she reached the door, she abruptly said, "Welcome back to La Femme De Coeur; I look forward to seeing you all in the hallways."

Then she was gone. Even though she was now gone, my heart continued to palpitate; this torment persisted until my piano class later that day. When I heard the sound of each key, it consoled me very much. The fear Madame Rosette had instilled in me was gone; the sound of the piano had made it all disappear.

The bell rang; we all went to the school eatery, where I sat with Clarisse, who was very happy to see me. She had returned with shorter hair; it suited her personality and character, I thought. Clarisse had shared with me her dreams of becoming a doctor, while I had not decided what I was going to do once school was over.

Clarisse asked if I had heard from Ethan.

I nervously replied, "No, at least not yet."

Clarisse looked away as if she knew something but was too afraid to share it with me. I panicked, not caring who noticed. "Clarisse, do you know something that you are not telling me?" I asked. "Because if you do, please do not leave me in the dark. I hated the dark side when I was a small girl, and you're only making me relive those dark days by silencing yourself, when clearly your lips are determined to tell me something."

Clarisse stood up and took a bite of her red apple. "I can't talk to you here, Judette," she said in a whisper. "Come to the school garden after school and I shall tell you everything I know."

Her refusal to not discuss the matter only aggravated the fear in my heart. I stopped eating and walked to biology, which was my next class. I could not concentrate at all, my mind was too preoccupied with what Clarisse had told me earlier. Somehow I managed to survive two hours of biology; it was now four in the afternoon. I proceeded to the school garden to meet Clarisse.

When I got there, Clarisse had not yet shown up. I sat impatiently on a chair outside the garden. I looked nervously at my watch; it was now twenty minutes past four. I tried to read my new biology book in order to calm my nerves, but that did not do any good. My thoughts still raced, and my heart feared what Clarisse was to tell me about Ethan. I hoped and prayed that Ethan was all right, even though his father had a very cruel heart.

I looked down on my watch again, when I heard Clarisse's voice.

I asked her, my voice sounding a little bit upset, "Where were you? It seems like I've been waiting here for you forever."

"I'm sorry," Clarisse said, looking in my eyes with a regretful look.

I said, "That's all right; now tell me what you know about Ethan."

Clarisse gave me another one of her bizarre stares, but I pretended to be brave, forcefully asking her to tell me what she knew about Ethan.

"Judette, I should have written to inform you that Ethan was not coming back here to the school, but I did not want to ruin your vacation. I figured you had a lot of things to catch up with, especially with the wedding of your sister. I did not think it would be appropriate to write to you about a boy you had obviously fallen hard for."

My own saliva choked me when I heard Clarisse tell me that Ethan was not returning; my stomach ached, and my head felt overcharged with defeat and rejection. I began to wonder if I had become like a character in a story, a girl who falls in love but is deprived of the object of her desire. I felt shattered. I managed to make Clarisse believe that I was fine when she asked if I was all right.

I paused in silence; after two minutes, I asked Clarisse, "Do you know why Ethan will not be coming back to school?"

Without hesitating, Clarisse gazed directly at me and answered, "It was his father's choice, Judette, not his own."

"Why is that? Why was it his choice?" I asked angrily.

"I don't know." Clarisse chose her words carefully; she continued, "I heard Alice and Elizabeth gossiping about this, and they said Monsieur Charles wanted Ethan to join the military and fight in the war, just like he had done."

I asked irritably, "But why would he do that? Why would he risk his own son's life by making him join the military, after everything he suffered in the war?"

Clarisse could not answer these questions. I couldn't blame her; I knew she had been innocent about all this. It wasn't her fault she did not know the answers; I could not understand Monsieur Charles's motive either. I knew very well my heart was shattered to hear that Ethan would not return to school, and I asked myself why Alice and Elizabeth had kept this information hidden from me.

I thanked Clarisse with a weak hug, following an empty smile; she knew I was not at all myself at this point. I found my way out of the school garden; when I got back to my room, I dropped into bed and turned off all the lights in my room. I couldn't see a single flash of light, everything became dark; I felt appeased by the absence of light. I tucked myself underneath the bed cover; although it was not cold, my skin shivered from the news I had just received. I could see nothing, feel nothing, and hear nothing except every beat my heart took from both pain and anxiety.

I finally made an effort to get up and wash my face in the bathroom. I could no longer be brave at this point; my eyes became soft yet very intense. Soon the tears fell endlessly from my eyes, I even tasted some of my own tears. I moaned, screaming from the bottom of my lungs. I could not get enough of my own tears, I wanted to cry, I wanted to scream, I wanted to shout and scream.

After crying in the bathroom for a good two hours, my bones felt weak. I thought a glass of water would do me good, if only I could find the strength to get up and get one. I never got the strength I needed to get a glass of water; I slept on the bathroom floor, until I felt rays of the sun flashing through the windows of my room.

I knew I had to write home and explain to Helene about what was going on with Ethan so she may pray for me. I thought that since she was very close to God, whatever she asked him on my part, he would surely grant. That morning, I wished I hadn't gone to school at all; I was feeling exhausted, my back was hurting, and my eyes were all puffy and red from all the crying I had done the previous night.

In the morning, I had mathematics with Madame Clementine; she was not as strict as the other teachers were. When I arrived in the classroom, I saw Alice and Elizabeth sitting next to each other; they were smiling when I entered the classroom. I was twenty minutes late, but Madame Clementine did not report me or send me to Madame Rosette's office, although she did tell me during class that I was one lesson behind and I needed to complete it.

I did everything I could to avoid Alice and Elizabeth. I wanted nothing to do with Elizabeth's sarcasm and Alice's nosiness. I knew them too well; they were both trouble. I was not one to judge others or blame others for my misery, but I always thought Alice and Elizabeth were not the type of girls one played with. They could fix you up or break you down into small pieces whenever they felt they were being double-crossed.

During lunch, I sat alone; I wanted nothing but silence. Elizabeth came over to the table where I sat. I glanced at her face and noticed that she had not changed a bit; her blue eyes sparkled with the intention to hurt someone's feelings, and her green skirt and her perfect white sleeveless shirt fitted her body very well. I always thought that while Elizabeth was not been blessed with a warm heart, but God sure did bless her with beauty like a goddess. She attracted a lot of attention from boys in the school, which generated envy and jealousy from other girls who did not have her beauty.

Regardless of Elizabeth's physical qualities, I wanted nothing more to do with her, especially now that Ethan was no longer a part of my life; I felt no desire to interact with her.

Elizabeth looked at me as if she was expecting me to say something, then she took the biscuit away from my hand and said, "Well, here's a girl who has disappeared since coming back from her vacation."

I tried to snatch the biscuit out of her hand, but she quickly moved away; she laughed and continued, "Not so rudely, Judette, I will give your biscuit back after you've told me why I haven't heard from you during these past few days."

I made another effort, and this time I managed to grab the biscuit away from her, telling her bluntly to back off. She began to clap her hands so loudly that everyone at the school eatery could hear her. Luckily, Clarisse came to my rescue just in time; she asked me if I was all right.

I replied yes, shaking my head at the same time, and then I pushed Elizabeth aggressively. "You knew!" I said. "You knew that Ethan had left the school to never return again, yet you paraded yourself as if it had little importance. I trusted you, yet you kept Ethan's departure a secret so my heart would keep pounding for him in both shame and misery."

Clarisse held both my hands, keeping me from making further agitations.

"I did not think you'd care, Judette." Elizabeth pierced my heart as she spoke these cold words. "I did not think it would matter even if he had left forever, even if he had died; after all he is just a tool, someone you kissed, isn't he?"

Elizabeth knew how to play with other people's emotions, using just her cruel words. She was very self-centered; she knew it was the fantasy of every boy at the school to become her love interest, but she never made an effort to treat any of them with respect.

Elizabeth continued to speak out in the open without any reservation to her tongue. "After all, I'm the one who introduced you to him, aren't I? If I had not felt sorry for you, I wouldn't have allowed him to even look at you even for a second; he only looked at you in the first place because I begged him to."

I grabbed her long hair and pulled her down onto the floor; I screamed with both anger and disgust at everything she had just said, pulling her hair and screaming out loud over and over, "I detest you! I loathe you, you hear? I loathe you, and I hope you're the one that gets killed before Ethan."

Before I could yell another insult at Elizabeth, I was snatched away from the fight by Madame Rosette. She took me to her office until I was able to calm down; she questioned me about my recent behavior and then told me to return to my other classes with a warning that if I got into another fight, I would be suspended for good. I skipped my classes and returned to my room, even though Madame Rosette had not suspended me. I wanted to be alone and reflect on what to do next. While I was in my room, Clarisse came to see me; she looked guilty even though I felt what had happened was not her fault. I always felt reassured by Clarisse's friendship; she never gave me a reason to doubt her. She always showed me compassion; she often came to me whenever I felt down, sad, or depressed, and I promised myself to do the same for her if she ever needed my help.

When Clarisse came into my room, I smiled at her; I did not expect her to come near me after the way I behaved in the school's eatery.

"I'm sorry," I managed to say, "I behaved like a fool, and I am sorry if I embarrassed you; I did not mean to behave in such a manner."

Clarisse quickly held me in her arms, and I felt more relief than I had felt since returning from vacation. We both shed some tears; mostly, I felt they were happy tears rather than sad ones. Clarisse looked like there was something more that she wanted to tell me. I asked her if everything was all right.

Her voice was breaking as she replied hesitantly, "I won't be back at La Femme De Coeur next year either. I just found out that my birth parents are still alive; they came to the school last month looking for me. My uncle, who raised me since I was of the age of two, had always told me that they died in a brutal car accident, and all of my life I have felt like I was not loved and appreciated enough. Now, well now, now what?"

I asked Clarisse to tell me everything and leave nothing out. "Well, now I think that I no longer need to live at the school, since my biological parents are here for me. They have been trying to speak to me, but I refused to see them when Madame Rosette sent me a letter last month while I was still enjoying my vacation at home. I had no interest in finding out who my real parents were, even though my uncle had advised me to find out more. I guess I owe it to myself, so I decided to go live with them at the end of this year."

I gave Clarisse a hug and told her I understood just how important it was for her to live with her parents and get to know them. I felt I needed to tell Clarisse about Anne, but I waited until the right moment came to tell her.

When Clarisse and I finished talking, I told her how much I appreciated her visit. "Clarisse, I must say your visit has been a comfort to both my mind and soul. Elizabeth and Alice were not at all who I thought they were, and I had not noticed all the negative things that were said about them since they came here. I should have listened, and maybe I would not be in the state I am in."

Clarisse's compassion always eased my sufferings. She said with reassurance, "It's quite all right; everyone makes mistakes, and we all tend to grow from each mistake that we make."

I had a necklace of Maman; I took it off my neck and put it in Clarisse's right hand, saying, "This is now yours; I am giving this to you, for you have shown me your loyalty even when I didn't fully deserve it, and I want you to take this necklace as a memory of our friendship."

Clarisse thanked me and left my room. I continued with my studies and went to all my classes. I worked harder than I had worked in years to save myself from disappointing Papa. The school year was hard, and then Helene wrote to tell me that Julie had suffered a miscarriage. I had called home to tell her that she could always try to get pregnant again; I wanted to reassure her that she was not under some curse or influence of witchcraft. I had been suspicious about the usage of witchcraft against her by those who did not want our family to prosper and be happy. I wanted to reassure Julie to not lose her hope in God.

Julie's miscarriage had not been the only bad news that I received; Helene also informed me of the death of Tante Gisela, who died in her sleep, and she was buried the next morning, just like she always wanted. Tante Gisela did not believe in the morgue. She always thought that mystery that was hidden in the morgue could not be comprehended easily. Tante Gisela had told my mother that some people conducted rituals using dead bodies at the morgue, and the water that they bathed the dead bodies with was used to enrich one's business, wealth, luck, health, power, and authority.

I imagined there must have been some truth to these beliefs of Tante Gisela, because she possessed a sharp wisdom when it came to protecting one against bad magic, witchcraft, and evil spirits. Her death left me crushed, but I was so grateful that we became friends and Tante Gisela gave me Maman's necklace.

Months went by, seasons changed, and Elizabeth and I had not made peace. I kept myself busy, practicing the piano, reading letters that Helene sent me, and writing to Papa when I wasn't in class or preoccupied with assignments.

Shortly before the school closed for the holidays, I couldn't wait to go back home and spend time with my brothers and sisters (Helene had become my sister also; I felt I loved her like one, and nothing could change that conception). One day while I was walking slowly down the hallway, I heard a noise, the type of noise that easily disturbs one's peace of mind. I did not care what others did, but I felt greatly disturbed by this loud peculiar noise. I held my books tighter to my chest and walked quietly through the hallway, attentively following where the screaming was coming from.

The loud cries and shouting were coming from Elizabeth's room, and her door was opened so wide that anyone passing by could clearly see inside. Elizabeth was being restrained by several teachers and Madame Rosette herself. She was kicking and screaming; she wanted to break free, but she couldn't because her arms and legs were being held tightly. When I finally saw her, her beautiful blue eyes looked red; it was as if she had been crying for a long period of time.

I was scared that someone would catch me spying, so I fled from there as soon as I could. I wondered what had happened to Elizabeth; her face looked unrecognizable; she did not even blink when I was observing her eyes. It was as if she had turned completely mad; if not, then something must have been very wrong because she was obviously not at all well. I had to find Clarisse; I needed to tell her what I had just seen. I went to the school garden, and Clarisse was sitting there on a bench.

She looked worried, just like I was. "What's going on, Judette?" she asked.

I took her hand and said, "Come on, we haven't got time to waste; it's about Elizabeth. I think she's not herself."

"And how do you know this?" Clarisse demanded.

"Well, I know, from what I have just seen, that Elizabeth is not fine; something is troubling her mind. She seemed agitated when I passed by her room; it looked as if she was being detained against her own wishes."

Clarisse exclaimed, "Oh my God, Judette, what if she's gone back to her old ways again?"

I asked, "What old ways?"

"Well, she gets that way every now and then." Clarisse said this and looked down her feet as we walked back to the school.

We went upstairs and headed to Elizabeth's room; we found out that she had already been taken someplace else. I needed Clarisse to help me find out where they had taken her. My hatred for Elizabeth soon turned into pity; I no longer wanted to find faults about her, I wanted only to see her and know for certain that she was going to be all right.

I said, "Clarisse, help me find out where they took Elizabeth, I must see her before they take her away."

Clarisse asked, "Since when has Elizabeth become your concern? Didn't you hate each other, and wasn't she so mean to you?"

I said, "Clarisse, my personal feelings have little importance; I need to see Elizabeth. I worry about her, and she probably knows where Ethan is right now and how I can communicate with him. After all, Elizabeth's family have greater wealth than anyone else in the school, and she knew Ethan before they came to La Femme De Coeur, and even if she does not know how I can reach Ethan, I only wish her well."

Clarisse shook her head. She said, "All right, I'll help you find out where exactly they took Elizabeth."

I said, "Clarisse, I do appreciate your help. I will always remember all that you've done for me in the past and continue to do."

Clarisse and I tried to search for Elizabeth without being caught or getting lost in the hallways. I was worried about what had happened to Elizabeth; she had made such strange screams in her room, I couldn't imagine why someone with her beauty would suffer so. Elizabeth was well aware of her beauty, and I always felt anyone walking in her shoes would have felt the same way. She knew how to find her way easily and get whatever she wanted or needed from any boy or girl. Her beauty made both sexes want to serve her or become her friend, not that she was very liked by many. Could it have been a charm? I couldn't answer this question myself; I had become more and more detached from Elizabeth's ways. I was fed up with how she wanted to run La Femme De Coeur School and turn it into her own image, but no matter how much I did not like her, I still needed to find her. I had to know what had happened to her, why the mean girl had suddenly lost her power.

Clarisse suggested that I go back to Madame Rosette's office and pretend to look for something; she told me that if I were lucky, I would hear them discussing Elizabeth's case, and that would give us an idea of what had happened to her.

I walked rapidly to the office, where I found Madame Rosette in a deep conversation with a tall man I had not seen in the school before. Their conversation was very discreet; I could barely hear what they were discussing, except when Madame Rosette demanded, in a very loud voice, to have Elizabeth immediately removed from the school before other students and parents became aware of her bizarre condition.

Madame Rosette's own words were, "I'm sorry, Monsieur, but it is not my responsibility or that of the school to keep Elizabeth here if her health requires mental treatment. I demand that you tell Elizabeth's parents that we won't be keeping her much longer; we will dump her on the street if they aren't here within twenty-four hours."

My heart felt a shock listening to Madame Rosette speak so heartlessly about Elizabeth. I thought, *What if it was me instead of Elizabeth? Would I be thrown out too, even though Julie is still my guardian? She has tried to take very good care of us ever since Maman left the world and Papa traveled* . I thought, *I cannot let Madame Rosette's evil ways paralyze me; I have to reach Clarisse as soon as possible and tell her what Madame Rosette said.*

I ran, catching my breath; the breeze on my face reminded me of the cold days I had experienced after Maman took her last breath. When I reached my room, Clarisse was waiting for me; I could always count on Clarisse when it came to loyalty; she was someone I could talk to and trust.

Clarisse nervously asked me, "What happened, Judette? Why are you running? What's going on with you?"

I could barely breathe; my heart was filled with palpitations of all types. I sat next to Clarisse and said, "It is worse than I thought; I did not hear everything, their conversation was very soft, too soft to distinguish what they were both taking about."

Clarisse stood up from her seat, wrapped herself with both her arms as if she was feeling cold and scared, and asked impatiently, "What is it that you didn't hear, Judette?" She added, "You are beginning to totally freak me out."

I did not respond right away; I waited to catch another breath, still wondering what would happen to Elizabeth if she was thrown out, and I became aware that none of us were safe at La Femme De Coeur. It was all just a big joke; our parents sent the school a big check every month in order for us to receive the best education ever, yet if a student fell into madness or folly, the school immediately bailed out on them. I felt the world was not strange, it was indeed the people who made the world a strange place to live.

I spoke again, this time making sure that Clarisse took seriously what I had to say. I grabbed Clarisse and shook her, and then I said, "We need to do something, anything, to help Elizabeth. I overheard Madame Rosette telling a man in her office that Elizabeth was to be thrown away on the street within twenty-four hours if her parents did not come pick her up."

Clarisse was as shocked as me when I first heard Madame Rosette's cold words involving Elizabeth's health. I sighed and then grabbed my sweater. I reached Clarisse's hand before we could waste another minute; I told her quickly, "Move, let's go," and we headed back to Elizabeth's room.

When we reached Elizabeth's room, it had been cleared out as if no one had ever lived there at all. I couldn't believe that Madame Rosette had done all this in a matter of a few hours. I had known she was vicious, but it wasn't comparable to what I was seeing now.

Clarisse looking very concerned. "What are we going to do, Judette?" she asked.

I said, "I don't know, but we'll figure it out together; we always have."

I tried to convince myself that it wasn't like when Anne had disappeared without a clue to lead us to her. Elizabeth was one of the most beautiful and popular girls in the entire school; if Ethan had told me that he had fallen for Elizabeth, I wouldn't have blamed him at all. I knew just how much every boy in my school was overpowered by her beauty. I knew I had to think, and I needed to think fast.

We walked out of Elizabeth's room and descended quickly down to the eatery; there was no one else there except for Monsieur Gaublet, who was one of the cooks in the school. I asked him with a desperate tone if he had seen Elizabeth.

He answered, looking rather detached and lost in his own little world, "No, Mademoiselle, I have not, but I heard the girl is mad; she has gone severely mad, there's no way for her to come back to her senses now. It's going to be a miracle if I see that happen."

I was weakened by everything Monsieur Gaublet said, but I managed to ask him, "Why do you think this, Monsieur Gaublet?"

"Well, I heard she has been in that condition for some time now, and the doctors have not been able to keep her appeased; it's a curse, a lot of people say, and Madame Rosette told me Elizabeth inhered her folly from her mother, Celine de Rose, who was both too rich and beautiful for her own good. I heard that her mother has been a mad woman ever since she was very young; she was luckily born from a very rich family; her parents owned property in five beautiful cities. They could get anything they wanted, except for their daughter to be normal just like any normal child. Elizabeth grew up with every doctor possible at her side, every day, monitoring her; it was very easy since they had all the money in the world to afford it.

"When Celine reached the age of nineteen, Monsieur Justin asked for her hand in marriage, but her father, Monsieur Jude Lorion, denied his proposal because they wanted to keep their daughter's mental illness a secret in order to preserve their family's name, image, and honor. When Elizabeth's mother reached the age of thirty, she became a burden to her parents, who had gotten old and could no longer take care of her, so they accepted Monsieur Justin's request to marry Celine.

"Celine's parents, Elizabeth's grandparents, wanted to make sure that their daughter would not be neglected if something ever happened to them, so they took the initiative to tell Monsieur Justin about her mental illness. When he learned the truth, his love for Celine ceased, and he became overpowered with both disappointment and regret, but it was too late for him to retreat from the marriage for he had already signed the paper of agreement. Luckily, immediately after they were married, she gave birth to Elizabeth, but her illness began to take over her. She once tried to suffocate Elizabeth with her own two hands, but one of her maids stopped her in time.

"After that, Monsieur Justin demanded to divorce his wife, but her father asked him to reconsider his decision; Monsieur Lorion offered to give him their entire wealth if only Monsieur Justin would agree not to divorce Madame Celine until death was brought upon one of them. Monsieur Justin, too greedy for the money, agreed; he stayed with Madame Celine."

I interrupted Monsieur Gaublet with a question before he even got the chance to start another sentence. "So you mean Monsieur Justin agreed to remain married to Madame Celine de Rose, so he could have her parents' money after they passed away?"

Monsieur Gaublet replied with a cough, "It wasn't just any amount of money, Mademoiselle; he was offered billions, and not only was he to become one of the wealthiest people in the world, he also became the owner of the properties that Monsieur Lorion once owned."

Then Clarisse asked, "So where is Madame Celine now?" She looked overwhelmed by what we heard Monsieur Gaublet tell us.

Monsieur Gaublet answered, "Oh, Madame Celine died after both her parents passed away; it was believed that Monsieur Justin poisoned her drink on New Years Eve. He denied all the allegations, of course, saying she was expected to die. He remarried just two months after Madame Celine died; everyone warned him that it was considered bad luck to remarry so soon, but he did not listen. He couldn't; the money he now owned took over his mind, his heart became cold, his actions cruel, and his words even bitterer than they were before."

Monsieur Gaublet continued, "When Monsieur Justin remarried, he never considered the possibility that his new wife would not like his daughter Elizabeth at all. His new wife, Madame Lila Francs, came with two daughters from a previous marriage; she had been married two times and each of her daughters had a different father. Monsieur Justin was now forty-two, and his new wife was thirty years old. Her daughters were the age of five and three. Monsieur Justin was always away on business, and during his absence, Madame Lila mistreated Elizabeth inhumanly.

"Monsieur Justin had informed Madame Lila that Elizabeth was born with an illness that demanded the most absolute care in order for it to cease its aggravation; he ordered Madame Lila to have doctors check her mind every three days. Madame Lila saw Monsieur Justin's request as unreasonable; she said that no child with madness should be allowed to waste other people's time, energy, and especially money, so she prohibited the doctors from visiting Elizabeth."

Monsieur Gaublet stood up from his seat and took a sip from his glass of lime juice. He stopped and then picked up where he had left. "Later on," he said, "Monsieur Justin came to learn that Elizabeth was neglected and mistreated every time he was away; he also learned that she had not been given any medication to moderate her illness. When Elizabeth reached twelve years old, she was sent to a place where she received special treatment for children in her condition. Her father made sure that she received extra care, since he had all the money in the world to do so, and he very much loved his daughter, even though people doubted that he loved her mother, Madame Celine, at all."

I asked irritably, "Well, if he loved Elizabeth so much, then why did he poison her mother?"

Monsieur Gaublet ignored my question and continued what he was saying. He continued, "Elizabeth received treatment for four years; when she got better, she returned home. Soon after, her stepmother passed away while giving birth to another daughter, who also passed away just two hours after she was born. Monsieur Justin grieved a lot after this; he couldn't get over the death of his wife and newborn daughter. Somehow he pulled out of the depression he was going through; meanwhile, doctors continued to visit Monsieur Justin's home; they wanted to be sure that Elizabeth did not go back to her previous state. When Monsieur Justin became too tired to take care of Elizabeth, he enrolled her here at La Femme De Coeur."

Suddenly, Clarisse said with a revolting voice, "How do we know that all this is not just a bunch of lies? Why should we believe you? After all, you are just a cook! How can we possibly trust you?"

"I am not asking for you to trust me," Monsieur Gaublet said aloud, sounding cold this time. "I am telling you what I know concerning Elizabeth, her illness, and her family. And if Madame Rosette was to learn that I was discussing any of this with you, I would surely get fired."

Then I said, "Then why did you never show Elizabeth any kindness or pity while she was here, if her family's history is as awful as you describe?"

"Don't get me wrong," Monsieur Gaublet said, lowering his voice, "Elizabeth is not a kind girl. I do not take pleasure in what's happening to her right now, but I know she was trouble to many girls in this school, and my faith indicates that God has a way from preventing evil from spreading worldwide."

I asked bluntly, "So you're basically saying, Monsieur Gaublet, that God is punishing Elizabeth with an illness of madness to prevent her from hurting others, is that it? One would think God is the God of compassion and that he will not give anyone such a terrible illness even if they've been bad or have done evil."

Clarisse's voice intruded, "What exactly are you saying?"

Monsieur Gaublet then said, "I don't know what I'm saying but I do know that everything that I have told you about Elizabeth and her family background is the infinite truth. I have nothing to lie about, and if you're here to see Elizabeth, you won't find her here in the kitchen with me. And if you're here to help her, I'm afraid you are too late."

"Tell us," I pleaded, "where is she? Where did they take her?"

Monsieur Gaublet bent over and whispered softly in my ear, "They couldn't reach her father ever since she's gotten ill again; the rumor is that Monsieur Justin died and left no will, which may leave Elizabeth with no aid whatsoever, while others say he has remarried and does not intend to take Elizabeth back."

"And what do you believe?" I asked, staring straight into his deep brown eyes, which were overshadowed by long eyelashes.

Monsieur Gaublet answered confidently, "I believe in neither story. I think this is all Madame Rosette's doing. As a new principal, she's very concerned about the school's reputation; she wants to be known as one of the best principals in the entire city, so I believe she would throw Elizabeth out and leave her in the middle of nowhere if her father does not come and get her."

I asked, "But why can't she call for Monsieur Justin to pick his daughter up?"

Monsieur Gaublet answered my question angrily, spitting accidentally on his shirt as he said, "She's scared the public will notice Elizabeth's madness, and as a result they may not want to have their children attend La Femme De Coeur."

Clarisse disgustedly said, "She is madder than Elizabeth is. She's the one who should be thrown out."

I asked Monsieur Gaublet, "How can we find Monsieur Justin?"

He replied, "My wife's parents were friends with Madame Celine's parents, and I learned all this from my wife, who grew up not too far away from where Monsieur and Madame Lorion lived. If you want me to help, you will have to wait until my shift is over; you can meet me outside the school at five o'clock."

I said, "Fine, we'll be there."

Clarisse and I went back to my room, where we waited impatiently for Monsieur Gaublet to finish working his shift. At five o'clock, we left my room and went outside the school, but we did not see Monsieur Gaublet. It was as if we had just missed him, but that couldn't have been accurate because we came on time. I told Clarisse, appearing more confident, that he'd be here soon, he was simply running late.

After waiting for several minutes, there was still no sign of Monsieur Gaublet. I became scared that something had happened or he had changed his mind. I thought that maybe he didn't want to help, since he feared getting fired if Madame Rosette ever found out that he had spoken to us about Elizabeth.

Clarisse and I waited patiently; the wind was getting colder, and my feet grew sore from standing. I looked at the clock ; it was after six . I had little hope to help Elizabeth and mend whatever was broken between us. Clarisse suggested that we go back to the eatery and see for ourselves what exactly was going on.

We made our way back to the school eatery; no one was there except for Monsieur Ange, who was Monsieur Gaublet's cooking partner. He looked as if something was troubling him. Monsieur Ange was nothing like an average cook, nor was he as social as Monsieur Gaublet. Monsieur Ange had been in the military, and he had lost an eye and a leg in combat. He had spent eighteen months in the hospital; by the time he was done with his treatment, he had lost all of his memories and he had to start anew.

When he got out of the hospital, he married one of the nurses who took care of him. I heard that he had been unable to move at all. His wife loved him very much, but five years later, she divorced him. He withdrew from everyone and became a cook in my school. He had been working in my school for over two years now, yet he spoke to no one, not even to those with whom he cooked our food.

Monsieur Ange sat on an old chair. I asked him softly, "Are you all right?" He gave no answer to my question.

I whispered to Clarisse, "Let's get out of here; I don't think he knows anything."

We began to walk out of the eatery; before we reach the exit, we heard Monsieur Ange say, "He's gone, gone forever."

I asked who, even though I knew who he was talking about.

He answered angrily, "Gaublet, of course."

He stood up; he did not add another word after that, and then he was gone. I knew we were out of time, but it was too late for me to do anything. All the hope I had stored for finding Elizabeth was crushed by what I had just heard. As much as I wanted to find out what had happened to Monsieur Gaublet, I couldn't help but feel my perseverance would not help me the least bit.

Monsieur Ange never talked to anyone, except when Madame Rosette asked him a question. Clarisse and I left the eatery and went to her room. I told her I was too depressed to go back to my room; I needed to be in a place where I had no recollections or memories of Elizabeth. Clarisse went straight to her books while I rested on her bed.

I slept for a good five hours; when I woke up, it was two in the morning and Clarisse was asleep. My throat was dry; I wanted water, so I took a glass. The coldness appeased the palpitation my heart was experiencing. I was worried about what would happen to me the next day. Ethan was gone, and I had no clue of what became of Elizabeth. I couldn't tell if she had been removed from the school or simply locked away in a dark room like a dungeon. I wanted to write home to Julie and Helene, but I stopped at once; I feared it was better that I cover all my trouble with silence rather than spread it to both Julie and Helene, who had enough to deal with at home.

Instead I grabbed Clarisse's biology book and began to read, just to let time pass by faster. At six in the morning, I had to wake Clarisse up, we both had classes beginning at seven o'clock. I made my way to the shower, and so did Clarisse; we both put our uniforms on and went to the school eatery for breakfast. After breakfast, we went to our mathematics class.

When I arrived in the classroom, everyone looked at me and began whispering. The teacher ordered silence in the classroom; regrettably, this order made matters worse. Alice was not one of the students whispering, but she did not look at all pleased (not that she ever did).

Clarisse took her seat and told me to ignore the whispering. After mathematics, I was to attend my Latin class; I had no strength to do so, but I could not miss a single class. I was in fear of being caught by Madame Rosette; I feared her total being. I didn't like what I heard her say about Elizabeth; I thought as wicked as Madame Rosette was, I should stay away from her scorn. My Latin class was quiet, no one spoke even once while I was there; noise was never tolerated in this class, Monsieur Gilbert was known to send students who did not obey to Madame Rosette's office, and every student feared being face to face with Madame Rosette.

After Latin class, Clarisse met up with me at the school eatery. I tried to talk with Alice, even though I knew she did not want to have a single word with me. She refused to even look at me. I wondered if she knew about what had happened to Elizabeth. After lunch was over, I went to my last class of the day, which was geography. I tried to be as attentive as I could; I had a exam coming in two days and had not studied or done my assignments. I did not want to repeat that class. Just before the end of the class, Madame Rosette came into my classroom. I trembled. She walked toward my teacher, Monsieur Albert, spoke in a very low voice, and then walked out.

When the bell rang, Monsieur Albert said, "Judette, I need to speak to you before you leave."

My teeth chattered at this idea; I wondered if Madame Rosette found out about Clarisse and me. Did she know that I had spoken to Monsieur Gaublet about Elizabeth? Did he tell her that I was looking for Elizabeth and wanted to help her? What would happen to me if I was expelled? I thought Papa would be so disappointed in me, and I couldn't take another one of his reproaches at this point.

I waited after class to talk to Monsieur Albert. Once he was done going through some papers in his hands, he said, "Madame Rosette wants you to meet her in her office; she has something really important to tell you."

His voice remained clear as he spoke to me, while he did not even try to give me the slightest gaze; meanwhile, I stared at him very attentively, making sure that I did not misinterpret a single word that he said to me. "Judette, I must tell you that Madame Rosette is not one who finds others very pleasant, no matter what the circumstances are. This is why I felt obliged to warn you she will interrogate you about everything you and Monsieur Gaublet spoke about in the last twenty-four hours, and I must warn you for your own very sake, my dear, that you protect yourself even if you have to lie."

I crossed my fingers really tight while sweat covered my face. I went from feeling cold to really feeling hot, and I did not know how to respond to what Monsieur Albert had just told me.

I stood politely and said, "Thank you, Monsieur Albert, for your concern. I spoke yesterday to Monsieur Gaublet about my concerns for Elizabeth. She did not seem too well the last time I saw her; she seemed to be close to madness."

Monsieur Albert approached me and wanted me to understand exactly what he was going to say. He said, "Now, you listen here, young lady. I don't know what you saw or heard Elizabeth do, but whatever you did see, you need to erase that out of your head; this matter does not concern you now or ever, and if you think you can interfere with the way Madame Rosette runs this school, then maybe you don't truly understand what you are getting into. I propose, for your own good, that you tell Madame Rosette of your innocence;

make sure you play things according to however she'd like, and whatever you choose to do in there, do not get smart with her, do you hear me?"

I fearfully replied, "Yes, Monsieur Albert."

He then said, not expressing any feeling on his face, like he had done before, "Now go."

I left Monsieur Albert's class and went to Madame Rosette's office; before I went in, I paused for a minute to calm my nerves, but that seemed useless at this point. When I entered Madame Rosette's office, her secretary was not at her desk. Before I could announce my presence, Madame Rosette called out my name.

I looked around and trembled at the sight of her long blondish hair; I did not know how to present myself, and so I said, "Monsieur Albert said that you called for me."

"Yes, Judette," she said with her face straight and her eyes not blinking at all, "sit down."

I said, "Thank you, Madame Rosette."

She said, "No need for you to thank me; by now, I am very much used to not hearing any words of gratitude from students, teachers, or those outside of the school."

I pretended not to understand what she meant by that; I held my bag in my arms close to my chest, even closer than I held it before.

I asked with my voice reserved, "What do you wish to tell me, Madame Rosette?"

She looked tense, and I made sure I said nothing more to disrupt her silence.

Then she said, "I called you here because of something that took place yesterday; it is a matter of great importance. It's about information that was shared yesterday against this school's policy, and I heard you were part of this conversation."

"I see," I said, leaning farther away from her as my fear increased.

"Judette, I have no intentions of sending you home, neither do I want whatever is discussed here today to spread out of this office; do you understand me?"

I said, "Yes."

"Yes what?" she asked strictly.

I said, "Yes, Madame Rosette, I understand nothing that is discussed here between you and I is to be spoken about out of your office."

"Good," she said, "I see you catch on quite quickly."

I said nothing to that comment. I sat still, not wanting to aggravate her tone more than it already was.

"You see, Judette, it is very important that you tell me everything that Monsieur Gaublet told you yesterday. If he is to return to La Femme De Coeur School, it is very important you say exactly what he told you yesterday about Elizabeth. I will not waste a lot of time over this matter; I have already done everything I could do to make sure that no one learns more about this, so it is now your responsibility to reveal the details of your conversation with Monsieur Gaublet. I must protect this school from lies and corruption, as I promised to do when I took charge of my position here."

I thought, *Oh God, Monsieur Albert had warned me of this.*

It was as if he had known about what was to happen to me; it was as if he had experienced in the past Madame Rosette's wrath himself. I told myself not to be afraid; it was pointless at this time. I hid my fears under a shell and managed to portray an image of bravery and sincerity so that Madame Rosette did not suspect my fear and discover that I was lying.

I pulled up my chin and said very gently, "Madame Rosette, I had no idea that Monsieur Gaublet knew Elizabeth personally or knew about her parents, and if Monsieur Gaublet spoke to someone about Elizabeth, it wasn't to me, because I never spoke to Monsieur Gaublet about anything before, or now."

Madame Rosette sighed heavily at this; she got up from her chair and threw me a suspicious gaze. I made sure I showed her no weakness or doubt on my part.

She then said, "All right, everything is fine; you may leave this office."

I stood up from where I was sitting and walked out of her office; she called out my name, but this time her voice wasn't as loud. She said, "Judette, you know no one can lie to me and get away with it, so if I find out that you have lied to me, I will have you expelled from the school and you will never be allowed to return; do you understand me?"

I said confidently, "Yes, Madame Rosette, I do understand."

I walked out from Madame Rosette's office. I was tired and needed to sit down and think things through, but before I could do that, I needed to find Clarisse and warn her about Madame Rosette's suspicions. I wished I could speak to Helene and tell her that I had gotten into trouble. I wished Helene could read my mind and tell me what I needed to do; maybe if Ethan was here with me, he could have helped, but Ethan had problems himself. I would have been the last concern on his mind, even if he had been here.

I went to find Clarisse in her room. She was laying down in her bed; she looked like she had been daydreaming. She got up from the bed and exclaimed with relief, "Judette!" She said my name as if she had been waiting for me for quite some time now.

I reached out to her quickly and hugged her; I thought she had probably heard about my visit to Madame Rosette, but I wanted to rest a little bit before I told her what had happened. My friendship with Clarisse had developed into a very loyal bond; her loyalty was like the reliability I received from Helene. Clarisse had sacrificed so much for me; even when Ethan had left school, it was Clarisse who had told me the truth, while Alice and Elizabeth kept their selfish mouths shut. I told myself that I had to protect Clarisse and be there at her side in case Madame Rosette came after her. I felt she deserved my friendship and loyalty; she had been there for me just like Helene had.

We held each other tight. As we hugged each other, I thought my fear was also Clarisse's; could it be that Madame Rosette had already spoken to her, or did she fear what would happen to me if I was expelled?

Pulling my arms away, I said, "Clarisse, there's something that I need to talk to you about right away."

Clarisse pulled away from me even further, as if she knew that whatever I was about to tell her could not possibly be good. My face looked troubled, and I had no makeup on (I had not used any since the day I found out that Ethan was not coming back); my face looked plain, but my pale skin added to the plainness of my face. I could really care less at this point. I had more important issues to worry about than how my face looked.

"Clarisse," I said, "you and I may be in more trouble then we assumed. Madame Rosette called me into her office after class today. My instinct told me that this was not good, because Monsieur Gaublet has been fired from his position here at the school. I have no clue what will happen to us if Madame Rosette pursues her investigation and finds out that we spoke to Monsieur Gaublet. The truth will not save us, but my lies will condemn us both and leave us without mercy under Madame Rosette's authority."

I reached out to Clarisse and walked toward her. She did not hesitate to put her hand on mine; her lips trembled, and her hands shook. Her face appeared red and her eyes even redder. I had not seen such vulnerability and fear in Clarisse before, and it scared me more than the situation we found ourselves in.

Finally Clarisse was able to speak. "What are we going to do, Judette? Nobody has ever stood in Madame Rosette's way; even if we lie today, she will still find a way to reveal the truth; no matter what she does in her heartless way, she will enjoy the pursuit of this matter more than any of us would."

Looking worried but focused, I said, "I know, Clarisse, this is why it's very important that you tell her that you and I know nothing of Monsieur Gaublet's betrayal; if she asks you about him, you must insist that we never spoke with him about Elizabeth."

Clarisse nodded her head and said, "Yes, yes, yes, I will do what I can to keep our conversation with Monsieur Gaublet a secret until we find out what they did to Elizabeth."

As Clarisse spoke, I thought again about whether Ethan could have helped us if he were still here at school. I was still angry at him; he had not written to me since he left. At times I wanted to burn all the notes he had written to me in the past, but I did not have the courage to do that. I did not want to lose the only thing that kept the memory of our conversation at the school garden alive. I wondered how he looked in his uniform.

I had hoped to receive information from Elizabeth about where Ethan was, but in the end, she proved to be of no help. I was desperate whenever I thought I might not ever see Ethan again, but I had to concentrate on what would happen if Madame Rosette ever found out that Clarisse and I had spoke to Monsieur Gaublet about Elizabeth. I reminded Clarisse to keep her mouth shut whenever she spoke with other students. I did not worry about Clarisse, for she had kept silent in the past whenever I said things I wanted her to keep to herself.

The next day came; Clarisse and I acted as if nothing had happened. We attended our classes and did not hear from Madame Rosette at all, which pleased us both very much. At the school eatery, students asked about what had happened to Monsieur Gaublet, but I ignored their questions in order to not attract any suspicions. Clarisse waited for me after school; we had made a promise to protect each other, and we figured the more we were together, the better off we were. When I saw Clarisse by my classroom door, she had a big smile, which she had not had for many days now.

I asked her what made her smile; she continued to smile even more. I said, "All right, if you're not going to tell me why you are smiling in the middle of the afternoon, then maybe I should ignore it."

She grabbed me and said, "Judette, it's Ethan!"

I said, "What?"

She sounded more excited than I had ever seen; she said, "I saw Ethan! He was dressed in his military uniform; he says he's in town for a week and wishes to speak with you as soon as possible. I told him you were still in class, and he agreed to wait. He said he was going to go for a long walk so time would not be still, and I promised him that I would find you and bring you to him in the garden."

My heart nearly fainted. "Are you kidding me?" I asked. "Is Ethan really here?"

"Yes, yes, yes," Clarisse said with insistence.

A part of me wanted to believe her, yet another part of me found this too difficult to believe. I said, "Please, don't play with my mind; it would be too cruel of you to do such a thing."

Clarisse took my hand and began to run. I had to hold on to her hand tighter; she was running too fast for me to keep up. My books fell, and I stopped to pick them up.

Clarisse screamed, "Hurry up! I'm sure he's already at the school garden waiting for you."

We reached the school garden. It was colder than ever; the roses no longer bloomed. The garden no longer carried the same beauty and life it had carried with it the last time Ethan and I were there. I stopped anxiously, hoping but doubting at the same time. I looked at Clarisse; a tear dropped from my eye. I became too emotional to see Ethan again.

I began to walk as fast as I could away from the garden. Clarisse grabbed me and said angrily, "Why do you run? Have you ever stopped to think that maybe Ethan wants you to want him? It is his father who holds him far and away from you and everything you both dream of."

I wasn't convinced; I thought about the pain I had experienced when I learned he had joined the military. As I turned to walk away, I bumped into a tall gentleman, and to my surprise, it was Ethan. Before I could open my mouth, he grabbed me with both his hands.

He said, "At last, I see you again, Judette."

I tried to hit him, I was so consumed with anger. I demanded, "Let go of me right now, I have no time for your empty words."

He grabbed both my hands and held me in his strong arms. I noticed how he had changed; he was even more polite than he had been when I last saw him, not that he was ever impolite.

Ethan softly kissed my red hair; it was as if that was the only thing he had wanted during all the time he was away. I thought if he wanted to kiss my hair, then he must have missed me a lot. My body gave in to his strength little by little; I surrendered in his arms, while he held me tight as if I was a little baby.

Then he said, "I have come with permission from my military officer; I needed to see you just once more before I departed for the war."

Clarisse smiled and said, "I want to give you both enough time to talk," and she walked away.

I looked in Ethan's eyes; they were as clear as a crystal. I wanted to tell him how much I had missed him, but I couldn't open my mouth. I grabbed him even closer and wept on his chest, not caring much about his uniform. I needed to release every emotion that I had battled with ever since I last saw him.

Ethan sat down on a bench in the garden, and I sat on his lap; we tried to find the right words to tell each other. Finally it was Ethan who spoke. He kissed the back of my neck and said softly, "I am very sorry, my love; I did not wish to cause you any grief or add more pain to your fragile little heart."

I answered, looking down at my skirt, "My heart is fragile but never too small to keep you in it all the time that you were gone."

I started to get up from his lap so I would have enough space to breathe and speak freely, for the closer I sat next to him, the more I wanted him.

He took my hand and pulled me back down on his lap; he started to kiss me as if he had waited all of his life for that kiss. We kissed for a good three minutes, and when he released my lips in order for me to catch my breath, I was amazed. I felt loved and comforted. I had many thoughts and feelings traveling my mind. I wanted him to kiss me again, and I wished that Elizabeth had been there to see him kiss me, but I knew it no longer mattered.

Ethan and I both stood up; he held my hand tightly and said, "It's getting cold."

I asked, "Do you want to go inside? I could fix us some hot tea to warm up our blood."

He responded softly, "That is a great idea."

We went inside the school; from there, we found our way to my room. When I got there, Clarisse was laying on her back and staring at the ceiling. Ethan took off his coat and placed it on a chair.

Ethan took a seat; his manners caught my attention and made me love him even more. I found that he had changed in everything he did, the way he walked and even the way he spoke to both Clarisse and me. While Clarisse spoke to Ethan, I fixed us three cups of tea. As we sipped our tea, we smiled in sincere silence until Ethan asked about Elizabeth.

Clarisse and I looked at each other when he mentioned Elizabeth's name. I was too frozen to respond to Ethan's question but Clarisse did. She said, "Yes, we've seen Elizabeth but not recently."

I thought, *Poor Ethan, if only he knew about Elizabeth and her drastic fate.* I wanted to tell him, but with everything that Madame Rosette had threatened us with, I was too afraid to even mention Elizabeth's name.

Clarisse added more tea to her cup and then asked Ethan, "So how does it feel to be in the military?"

Ethan smiled at that question; he took my hand in his and then said, "One feels lonely most of the time because the one he loves is too far away for one to reach and hold."

After Ethan said this, I stood up. I remembered how empty, angry, and confused I had felt for months after he left to join the military. I put down my cup and asked Ethan, "Does one get so lonely that one fails to send a word or write a love letter to the one his heart claims to desire?"

Ethan walked to me and grabbed me from the back; I felt for once that he was trying, and I felt his love and desire to be with me.

I then asked, "When will you return from the war?"

His face filled with disappointment, and he replied, "I'm not sure when, my love."

He continued to hold me while Clarisse looked happy to what she was seeing. It was now past seven; Clarisse wanted to return to her room, so I asked Ethan to walk her back while I changed from my school uniform to my night gown.

Ethan and Clarisse were gone a few minutes; after he returned to my room, I asked him if Clarisse got to her room all right, and he said very briefly, "Yes, and I asked her to lock her door."

I grabbed Ethan's hand and rubbed it on my left cheek. Ethan took me quickly in his arms, where I felt I belonged forever; he lifted me up and tucked me into bed, and I once again felt safe.

He then asked me, "How is your family?"

I said, "Julie had a miscarriage, and I wrote to her in order to console her. I asked her not to give up her hope but to instead try once more, and hope that God finds a way to help her and Robert. How about you?" I asked, looking right at his face.

"Well," he said, "I wanted to come back and ask your hand in marriage once you were done with school, but that dream crashed with my father's demand for me to join the army."

I asked, without holding myself back, "Then why did you not refuse?"

He said, "It's not always easy to refuse a parent's wish. I tried to do just that, but he is as cold as a dead body inside the morgue. My father knows no pity, he only knows all the battles he fought during war and wants to see that I continue as his son to carry out the family's name in honor."

I looked down hopelessly; what Ethan said wasn't anything new, but I was not angry this time. I understood it wasn't Ethan's choice to be separated from me, it was his father's selfish desire to have him join the military.

Ethan was about to leave; it was now nine in the evening. As much as I wanted Ethan to stay, he and I knew he had to leave. One of the rules at La Femme De Coeur was that boys and girls were not to be in the same room after eight, and it was now nine.

After Ethan left my room, I turned off my light, and just when I was about to close my eyes and fall asleep, I heard Ethan's voice say, "I can't go home alone; either you come with me or I'll spend the night with you here."

I knew Ethan was not going to leave my room; I thought fighting would not do any good. He took off his jacket but kept his shirt and pants on. Ethan and I spent the night in each other's arms; all night I felt his warm breath on the back on my neck. He held me tight and very close to him; it felt as if he would never let go of me, and I liked that because I did not want to let go of him.

A knock at the door woke us up around seven in the morning; I was worried about who it was and made Ethan hide underneath my bed; when I opened the door, I was pleased to find that it was Clarisse. She had come very early to get me to go to our first class of the day. I made her enter, and she gladly did.

She asked, "Where's Ethan? I know he did not go home."

Before she could say more, I called out, "Ethan, Ethan, it's okay. Come on out, it's just Clarisse, who wanted to make sure that I did not miss my class."

Ethan came out looking more handsome than ever; his eyes were clear and bright; his white T-shirt showed how beautiful and well formed his entire body was. I blushed and looked away. I went to the bathroom, where I brushed my teeth and took a bath.

I put on my uniform and came out and kissed Ethan on his cheek. Clarisse and I left for our morning classes. At lunchtime, Ethan met us at the eatery; he brought me fresh roses. I took them from his hand gently.

He said, "I have to go home and do some work for my father."

I asked disapprovingly, "What type of work would that be?"

He did not answer my question; he said, "I'll return before you even know it."

Ethan left, and I went along to my other classes. Clarisse and I still had not heard anything from Madame Rosette; as much as we loved not hearing from her at all, we were still concerned, for we did not know what was ahead of us,

When my classes for the day were done, I wanted to write to Julie and Helene, so I grabbed my pen and paper, and I began to write. When I was done, I went to mail both letters. When I returned from mailing my letters, Ethan was waiting in my room. I was happy that he had kept his promise.

Ethan and I drank tea and practiced the piano together; when we were done playing the piano, we danced *a little.* I floated in my long violet dress that Julie had given me as a present when I had gone back home for vacation. Ethan and I read to each stories from old books; when we were done entertaining ourselves, I took a blanket from my suitcase and offered it to Ethan.

I said, "I hope this keeps you warm and reminds you of me wherever you go."

Ethan said, "I need no blanket to remind me of you, for you live in my heart for eternity."